WHAT OTHERS ARE ! 2ND EDITION OF THE

C000049478

"There are very few best reads specific to our industry that are dead on with issues we face today. Each year I provide The Dealers Voice to our sales team to provide them with the most relevant and current insight to today's business. Our team shares this with our customers to help them deal with the business challenges we face."

- Mark E. Legget, Former VP of Sales, Kraftmaid Cabinetry

"I make sure I have an extra copy of The Dealer's Voice to give to my dealers because I know they can financially benefit from the information provided within."

- Simon Solomon, President, Ultracraft Cabinetry

"This contains solid fundamentals of running a highly profitable cabinet operation in a clear and concise format. The Dealer's Voice is easy to understand and I find the best practices highly effective after our dealers implement them."

- Steven Nash, VP of Sales, Armstrong

"This book covers more than just best practices. It also covers emerging techniques dealers can use to streamline their operations. What I love about it is that the topics are based on hundreds of dealership studies—not just one."

- Carlos Ansoategui, VP of Sales, Legacy Cabinets

"There's a great need to share this kind of information with dealers who are currently struggling in today's market. I sincerely hope every dealer by now has bookmarked http:// dealersvoice.companioncabinet.com as their first stop after a fresh cup of coffee in the morning."

- Miguel Merida, President North America, Autokitchen, Microcad Software

"CompanionCabinet truly understands our industry and has a depth of knowledge that can only be gained through many years of experience and living it on a daily basis. In times like these it is important to have this experience working for your team."

- Joe Jacobus, President, Markraft Cabinets

"There is no other place you can find this information— the subject matters are so in depth and in sync with what is actually going on in our industry. The Dealer's Voice is a must read and every dealer should have a copy of this in their library."

- Joe Demussi, President, Direct Cabinet Sales

"It's amazing to me that so many practical ideas can be presented in one book. It's obvious that these articles were written by experienced cabinet industry individuals who have lived what we live on a daily basis."

- Bryce Maryfield, Owner, Arrowwood Cabinetry

"The concepts behind these articles are innovative and refreshing. Anyone related to the cabinet industry could pick up this book and get something out of it that would be incredibly helpful to them. The level of detail is fantastic."

- Tony Picciano, VP of Sales and Marketing, Modern Builders Supply, Inc.

"Just the sales process portion of this year's edition is an absolute must for every cabinet dealer. I can forecast much more easily and our designers and management staff finally speak the same language. The best part is we close more effectively and have happier customers now."

- Doug Haynes, CEO, Kitchen Art

"The Dealer's Voice represents the collective knowledge from the most successful aspects of every dealer's operation. While reading this on a plane ride, I realized things I could improve about my business the very next day."

- Brad Schrock, Owner, KitchenLand USA

"I've always believed in the value of great content, provided it is specific and relevant to its audience. The Dealer's Voice not only delivers great content to cabinet dealers and manufacturers, but it also provides valuable lessons learned that every dealer should know."

- *Doug Krainman, Publisher, Kitchen and Bath Business Magazine*

THE DEALER'S VOICE

Second Edition

Why Some Cabinet Dealers Make Money ...and others don't

A Series of Published Articles
CompanionCabinet Software

ISBN - 1439271836
ISBN-13 - 9781439271834

Contents

Dear Friends,

This year we've included twenty-one articles. These articles contain information on how to structure your sales process, how to help your salespeople close additional sales, how to develop strategies for survival and controlling costs, and how to use targeted automation to improve a dealership's bottom line. These articles are based upon the experiences my family and friends have had over fifty plus years in the cabinet industry. I hope the information provides value to you.

Readers of *The Dealers Voice* can increase the value of this publication by sharing it with their co-workers and discussing how the ideas contained in the articles can be applied in their situation. If you would like to receive these articles periodically, please register for notifications of new content at http://dealersvoice.companioncabinet.com/register. We are always looking for new authors. If you would like to contribute to our growing community, contact us at dealersvoice@companioncabinet.com.

A special thanks to the many dealers that have shared their secrets of success with me over the years. I have had the privilege of visiting dozens of dealers each year during the twenty-two years I have spent in the cabinet industry. The secrets they have shared with me serve as the foundation for many of these articles.

Also a special thanks to the staff of CompanionCabinet Software. You'll notice some new authors in this year's edition. Their deep industry knowledge, street smarts, and editing skills have been priceless as we've expanded the breadth of topics we write about. Without their help, we would have never been able to present so many practical business ideas in such a clear and concise style.

The Dealers Voice is published annually. The information contained in the articles reflects the state of the industry when the article was originally published. The date each article was published appears at the top of the page.

Welcome to the 2nd Edition of *The Dealer's Voice.* And thank you once again for being a reader.

Sincerely,

Brent Jackson

President, CompanionCabinet Software, LLC

About The Dealers Voice

The Dealer's Voice started as a book of best practices for cabinet dealers. The articles are based on site visits and operational reviews from hundreds of dealers across the nation. CompanionCabinet Software published the book to help educate dealers on more profitable ways to run a cabinet operation.

The Dealer's Voice became so popular that it was expanded to a free online learning center located at http://dealersvoice. companioncabinet.com. It now includes best practices on virtually every aspect of running a highly profitable cabinet operation.

At CompanionCabinet's Fast-Track Dealer Summit in 2008, cabinet dealers identified sales as their most pressing challenge as they began the transition away from a builder-focused model to a balance of retail and other customer segments. In response to this, we interviewed over fifty of the top performing kitchen designers in our industry. We asked ourselves the question "What are they doing that enables them to drive such high volumes of revenue?"

The answers are contained within these pages and also within our latest addition to *The Dealer's Voice*—an audio broadcast that anyone can listen to from their browser, iPhone, iPad, iPod, iTouch, or on iTunes. It's called "The Dealer's Voice Podcast" and is free to anyone who registers on http://dealersvoice.companioncabinet.com/register.

We hope you'll take time to listen to these podcasts as our latest major edition to *The Dealer's Voice*. They are an easy way to get you and your staff more focused on how to be just as successful as the naturals in our industry.

Sincerely,

-The CompanionCabinet Team

NASA Required for Cabinet Dealership Accounting Implementation

2008/8/12 This headline seems ridiculous doesn't it? But cabinet dealers who tried tracking purchases of a semi-custom cabinet line in their traditional accounting system describe the experience like a failed moon-shot. Tons of nasty technical challenges, lots of creative "work-arounds" and then on launch day, the system impressively comes to life only to explode before it leaves the atmosphere.

Why?

Let's Start Simple

From a technical standpoint, the failed launch is caused by the differences between configured and non-configured products. Semi-custom cabinets are configured products. The buyer selects from a number of different options to get the exact kind of cabinet they want. Non-configured products are like stock cabinets. The buyer picks from a limited selection of products and the manufacturer produces them in one way only.

Accounting systems are set up to deal with non-configured products. Loading an inventory system with all the non-configured products the dealer sells is more of a labor challenge than a technical one. Here's a quick summary of the steps a dealer would go through to load non-configured products into an accounting system:

- Accounting system's inventory module is loaded with SKUs (a.k.a. product codes), descriptions, and costs, all of which should be easily obtained from suppliers
- Employees key in product codes on a sales order after selling items
- Purchasing converts sales orders into detailed purchase orders for order placement
- Revenue flows into the G/L from the sales order and cost flows into the G/L from the purchase order with all the detail needed
- Management enjoys reports on cost of goods sold and other financial data it needs to manage the business

Houston, We Have a Problem – Configurable Product

If dealing with non-configured products is a "model rocket launch" for accounting systems, then dealing with configured products is like "colonizing Mars." Configurable products are made-to-order and dynamically customized or configured by the customer. Each configuration has a different cost associated with it. And these costs vary dramatically. This causes problems for traditional accounting systems, which depend on static lists of product codes to track revenue and costs.

Imagine the challenge when the accounting system tries to handle the configurable product line in a traditional manner. One choice is to glaze a cabinet (15 percent up-charge), while another choice is to add a rollout tray ($250 charge). We have one product (the cabinet) and two options (the glaze and the rollout tray). This means the accounting systems need a static list of four SKUs in order to match cost to sales quickly. The four combinations are:

- Cabinet only
- Cabinet with glaze
- Cabinet with rollout tray
- Cabinet with glaze and rollout tray

As the number of options grows, so does the need for NASA engineers. The engineers are required to tackle the technical challenges created by the length of the static list. The length of the list grows exponentially as options are added. The more choices you have, the more product combinations possible and the less capable a traditional accounting system becomes in dealing with all the data.

So when your local accounting software guru tells you he can handle your semi-custom line in the new accounting system he wants you to buy, ask him one question. "Which is greater, the number of SKUs needed to deal with our semi-custom line or the number of stars in our galaxy?" Unfortunately, the truth is, the number of required SKUs is far greater than the number of stars in our galaxy.

If you want a truly humbling experience, go to a secluded spot the next time the night sky is clear and gaze at the stars. Now visualize multiplying each star you see by millions upon millions. That imagery should help you appreciate how many SKUs are needed to deal with a semi-custom cabinet line.

Now think of your staff creating and maintaining all those "stars" and how your server will slow down as your accounting system desperately searches for the right "star" among all those different options. I think you'll come to appreciate why even very bright people fail when they attempt to use traditional accounting systems to track configurable products.

Unfortunately, the sad reality is that the brute-force approach to solving the configurable product challenge doesn't work. But what does?

Come On, Everyone Knows Size Really Matters

I remember my college girlfriend telling me that the size of the cabinet dealership I might own one day really didn't matter. Well, when it comes to dealing with configurable products it does, trust me. Smaller dealerships should ignore the inventory module of their accounting system and use paperwork to replace its function. The paperwork will be labor intensive, contain errors, and be difficult to manage; however, at lower sales volumes, paperwork is very cost effective.

But strange things begin to happen when there are more than five sales people.

The volume of revenue five or more salespeople generate starts to break the paper processes down. The day gets consumed by looking for lost paperwork, correcting errors, and retyping data into different systems. What is needed at larger dealerships is automation that sits at the front end of the process and organizes the data in a way that a traditional accounting system can handle.

Such systems simplify dealing with configurable products by using a more generic grouping combined with descriptor techniques to create "SKUs" for the accounting system with the correct cost and sell amounts. Such systems reduce labor and product costs as well as improve financial reports.

Rocket Fuel is Really Expensive

Manufacturers have spent millions upon millions tackling these challenges with the largest software and consulting firms in the world. And while they might end up with a solution at some point, the dollars being spent are staggering. So before you think, "Yeah, but I'm different," talk to other cabinet dealers who have attempted solutions on their own; not the owners—I mean the people actually using the system on a daily basis. Once you do that, you'll count your lucky stars that you did the research first before inadvertently authorizing hundreds of thousands of dollars in sunk costs on your own Mars colonization program.

2

Your Winning Season

2008/8/20 Pat Conroy's book, "My Losing Season" chronicles his senior year at college when he played point guard for the Citadel. He tells the story of a team with talent but no ability to create the team cohesion required for them to produce a winning season. The similarity between this team and many cabinet dealers is striking.

I think of business as a game. If I play the game well, my business prospers. If I play the game poorly, the business fails. Since I think of business that way, I see teamwork as a critical aspect of achieving success, and it surprises me how few cabinet dealers focus on getting the whole company involved in winning the game.

My four brothers and I use to play basketball. My oldest brother could kill any of us playing one-on-one. To make the game fair, we used to have two or three of the younger brothers play against him. When the younger brothers played as a team, we could beat him just about every time. However, there were times when my second oldest brother would try to prove he was as good as my oldest brother. He stopped passing the ball and would take a majority of the shots. We usually lost when that happened.

When I was running a cabinet dealership, I saw the competition as being like my oldest brother. It is bigger, stronger, and quicker than I am. So when I tried to figure out how to compete, I remembered the lesson I learned from my second oldest brother. I would lose if I made it all about me; I had to get the whole company involved to win against a bigger, stronger, and quicker competitor.

I have asked hundreds of cabinet dealers about how they get their teams involved, and four techniques seem to be common among those dealers who were getting the best results. The techniques are:

- Sales incentives
- Departmental and company bonuses based on profit
- Posting results publicly
- Team celebrations

Most cabinet dealers are using the first technique. Paying commissions is common in our industry. However, there are many different ways people pay commissions. The most effective way I have seen is to pay a variable percentage of the gross profit margin of the job, the commission percent being higher if the gross profit margin is higher. This technique aligns interests. The larger the amount of gross margin produced, the more the salespeople and company make. Accurate cost tracking is the real trick here.

Many cabinet dealers struggle with paying on gross profit margin because they do not have an accurate way to capture their gross profit margin by job. To do so requires them to have an accurate measure of all the costs by job. Their lack of systems allows costs to slip through the cracks, not getting allocated to the correct job. So when a salesperson forgets to include the agreed upon hardware when he prices the job, and then rush orders it after the customer complains, that cost never gets tied back to the correct job. A centralized purchasing function will help you solve this challenge.

The second strategy is departmental and company bonuses based on profit. Sales incentives gets salespeople motivated to drive more gross margin to the business, now use profit sharing bonuses to get the rest of the team motivated to drive down costs and drive up productivity.

The challenge to making this technique effective is making sure you tie incentives to both department level and company performance. For instance, an average warehouse mistake costs you $250 to fix. So a good warehouse incentive is based upon the number of deliveries a month (productivity) that are correct and damage free (cost related).

Purchasing staff can receive incentives based upon the number of POs placed (productivity) with no errors (cost). Service people can be paid an incentive based upon the number of jobs completed (productivity) in one trip (cost). Small improvements can result in big changes in profits when you realize the average service trip costs a cabinet dealer $200 (when you DON'T have to replace damaged or incorrect product).

When cabinet dealers are setting up these incentive programs, they often worry that the incentives will encourage one department to improve their performance by creating more trouble for another. I have a simple solution. Make 50 percent of the total bonus paid based upon department performance and the other 50 percent dependent on meeting company goals. Employees quickly learn they make the most money by improving departmental performance while meeting company goals.

Performance visibility is a key in this whole process. The department and company performance should be posted in a public area for all employees to see. You will be amazed at how focused on improvement your staff becomes when everyone can see how well or poorly each respective department is doing.

The information serves as feedback, which becomes the driver of team work. Each individual is clear on their role within the organization and has a clear idea of how each department and the company is progressing on their goals. This gives all staff members the information they need to make improvements on how they do their job and how they can help other departments improve on their performance. This data helps eliminate "turf wars" and encourages cooperation between departments.

But knowing all this information is not enough. Team cohesion is built during times of celebration. Structuring celebration events is the fourth team building technique. Most people go to work every day to get a paycheck. When employees are just showing up for a pay check, they usually spend their time trying to figure out how little work they can do and still get paid. Recognition, appreciation, and camaraderie are the catalysts that turn these sloths into valued contributors.

Team celebrations should be both small and large. A great opportunity for recognition is during monthly business reviews. Awarding a traveling trophy to the best performing department is a great first step. Bigger awards, such as a free day off, can be awarded for a significant quarterly achievement. A company outing at an amusement park is a great award for achieving an aggressive annual profit goal. Big and small, these celebrations create memories that connect employees with one another and help reinforce the concept that business success results in good times for the employees.

If you like these concepts but are skeptical if they really pay off, I encourage you to read Jack Stack's bestselling book, *The Great Game of Business.* Jack Stack is the CEO of SRC Holdings. In 1983, he bought a failing division of International Harvester and applied the principles I share with you in this article. His success is impressive. An investment of $10,000 in SCR Holdings then, is worth $5.5 million today. I think that is a really good payoff!

3

Organizing Salespeople for Success

2008/10/17 The cabinet industry is filled with stark contrasts, and nowhere in the industry is the difference between success and mediocrity as vast as in the sales arena. Some new salespeople get up to speed in a few months, others take two years, and still others are never really successful.

The best salespeople sell up to $4 million per year, while the poorer performers might only sell $200,000. Some of the variations can be explained by differences in markets, products, and types of customers served; however, in working with over one thousand cabinet salespeople over the years, I found the real reason for the differences boils down to one key issue—organization.

Salespeople are notoriously disorganized. They often remind me of my son. He is ten years old, full of enthusiasm and wherever he goes, a pile of toys lay in his wake. But when he wants to play outside, he often spends twenty minutes looking for his shoes. Over the years, I've tried to help him by adding more structure. Now might be the time you should help your salespeople by adding a little more organization to their life so they don't spend twenty minutes looking for a file every time a customer calls.

Over the years, I have developed a system that helps salespeople with organization. This system is comprised of three areas:
1. Capturing
2. Planning
3. Following Up

To start, the salesperson will need to go to the office supply store and buy a 250 page lab book, plastic inbox/outbox trays, a thirty-one-day expandable folder and a twelve-month expandable folder. The whole package won't cost more than $20.

Capturing

All salespeople's work comes from one of three sources—conversations, email, and or physical documents. The system I share with you uses the lab book, email folders, and trays as tools to help salespeople capture all their obligations in consistent places so that when they take time to organize their commitments, it is fast and easy to find all of them.

The process is simple. Have the salespeople keep their lab book with them at all times. Any time a customer requests additional work, the installer calls for another filler, or the superintendent calls about rescheduling an installation, the conversation should be recorded in the lab book. All action items or commitments should be starred or highlighted so they can be easily found.

Next, better organize their e-mail. Educate your salespeople on the value of adding folders to their inbox. Sources whom the salesperson gets e-mail from frequently, like a superintendent or e-newsletter from a manufacturer, should have their own folder. In addition, folders named "delegated" and "planning" should be added. Next, use your e-mail software's rules or filters to have e-mail from the frequent contacts automatically routed into their respective folders. The main inbox should only contain e-mails that the salesperson needs to read and act on. For many salespeople, this is like giving up crack cocaine. They must get to the point where if an email does NOT require action, it does NOT need to be in their inbox. It should be filed in an email folder for reference.

Another note on email—many salespeople get too much junk mail (non-work email). The amount of junk email increases over time, and every junk email that has to be looked at is a chunk of a salesperson's time. Have your administrator get a sense of how much non-work email is being received. Find a good junk email filter system. Some dealers even change a salesperson's email addresses periodically so that they can control this type of time-waster.

The plastic trays provide salespeople with a single place to put all the paperwork they receive. The trays serve the same purpose as the shoe rack by the door where my son always keeps his shoes. It is a single place where all installer punch lists, designs that need to be reviewed, and measurement notes are stored. Any document telling the salesperson to do something should go in the inbox tray until they review it in their planning time. Documents currently being worked with should be stored in a file on the salesperson's desk. Completed work should be in the outbox tray.

Planning

This next part requires discipline. Two or three times a day, the salesperson should spend up to thirty minutes planning. This involves reviewing all the new commitments they recorded in their lab book or received in their e-mail or inbox tray and organizing them for completion. The key to success is decisiveness.

The salesperson should go to their lab book, e-mail, and inbox tray and review all their new commitments. Not all these commitments are the same. Some will take little effort to complete; others will take hours of focused effort.

If a follow-up call, response to an e-mail, or verification of a customer's kitchen measurements takes under two minutes to complete, the salesperson should do it right then. A quick response to an e-mail and short calls should be taken care of during this thirty-minute planning session.

The salesperson will then have two types of tasks left. A set of tasks that can be delegated to others and tasks that need focused time to complete. Completing a kitchen design and taking measurements are good examples of tasks that need focused time set aside for their completion.

Encourage your salespeople to delegate anything that doesn't directly contribute to new sales (e.g., service follow-up activities, any type of investigation work, job status inquiries, scheduling issues, etc.). Most salespeople's sales production is limited due to their poor delegation skills. Remind the salesperson that if they are going to be successful delegating, they need to be clear about what the task is, the time and date of any interim follow-up, clarity about when the task is due, and what the result is when the task is successfully completed.

Salespeople also have a tendency to be over optimistic about how much work they can get done. Here's a little trick that I use to help them keep on track. When the salespeople review their commitments, I tell them to estimate how long it will take them to complete the task if they have no interruptions. Then, when planning to complete the work, I insist they book only 50 percent of their time to planned activities.

Why? Because no one in the cabinet industry has more than twenty minutes of uninterrupted time, and interruptions cost the salesperson 50 percent of their focused time for planned activities.

Follow Up

So now the salesperson has looked at their lab book, email, and inbox tray and either completed the task, delegated, or planned for doing the work themselves. What's missing? Follow up. Good follow-up is how the salesperson avoids spending their entire day fighting fires.

Providing a good follow-up system is where expandable file folders come in. During the daily, thirty-minute planning sessions, the salespeople should keep a pad of paper with them. As each task is either delegated or planned for later, the salesperson should drop a note in the slot of the thirty-one-day file folder corresponding to the date the salesperson is to start the task. Place the note in the slot of the twelve-month folder that corresponds with the month the work should start if the start date is more than thirty-one days away.

Every Sunday night, the salesperson should review their schedule and thirty-one-day file folder to review the week's commitments. At the end of every month, the salesperson should pull all the following month's information out of the monthly expandable folder and organize it into the thirty-one-day folder. The notes for work that has been completed should be thrown out and any related e-mail should be moved to an archive folder from the "delegated" and "planned" folders on the salesperson's computer.

This is called a "tickler file." It allows the salesperson to forget about the commitment once they file it, knowing they will be automatically reminded of it when they get to the day it was assigned. It keeps everything nice and clean and gives the salesperson more selling time, not to mention less stress from trying to keep all the commitments in their heads.

Conclusion

There you have it. Most studies say the average executive manager loses over an hour a day just looking for paperwork. I don't know about you, but many salespeople I have worked with are much less organized than a manager, so there's no telling how much time a disorganized salesperson loses. And when a salesperson is disorganized, most of their stress comes from emergencies and issues that bite them later from the disorganization itself.

With a little discipline and this system, you can help your salespeople gain back most of their wasted time and sell more of your products and services. In addition, you can help them have a better quality of life from the reduced stress level.

4

Should You Centralize Purchasing?

2008/10/28 The year 2009 looks like it will be another year of slow sales growth. The dealers I talk with tell me that there are still too many new homes for sale, builders are cautious, and sales of existing homes are slow. A few of the dealers have told me they have noticed a little more action in kitchen remodeling, but they quickly add that this trend is still more interest than actual buying.

Years like this are when astute cabinet dealers take a closer look at their operations and find new ways of doing business that reduces cost and gets more productivity out of their people. Over the years, there has been a debate about centralized vs. decentralized purchasing. Fans of centralized purchasing think it's a good way to get extra sales time inexpensively.

Traditionally, most dealers have had their salespeople do their own purchasing. This way of doing business started back when the owner founded the company. He or she designed the kitchen, ordered the products, coordinated the delivery, and even collected the bill. When it came time to add more salespeople, they just followed the owners lead.

As the sales teams get bigger, most dealers begin to have delivery coordinators and accounting staff free up salespeople's time by making someone else responsible for kitchen installation and collections. The salesperson spends less time doing what they don't like—pushing paper—and more time doing what they like, selling. It works out great for everyone.

Many dealers are slow to apply the same logic to purchasing. Let's say you have a sales team of five salespeople, all of whom spend 20 percent of their time filling out and placing purchase orders. For the price of a purchasing agent, you can get a salesperson and two thousand hours of selling time back. Even in a tough sales market, that's a good deal.

Most companies who centralize purchasing have the salesperson or associate do the kitchen design and prepare the quote for the prospect. After the quote is approved is when things begin to change. The salesperson in the centralized purchasing environment will create a job packet and send the information to the purchasing agent.

The purchasing agent is responsible for reviewing the design, organizing the required materials by supplier, and then creating and placing the purchase orders. Some variations exist, but for the most part the purchasing department also receives and checks the manufacturer's confirmations and enters the cost information into the accounting system.

The purchasing person becomes the point person for the salesperson on order status questions. Back-orders, anticipated delivery dates, modifications to the orders, and rush orders are all handled by the purchasing person. The purchasing person takes on a lot of paper and follow-up work that normally robs salespeople of their selling time.

Building supply companies and cabinet dealers with multiple locations can centralize purchasing as well. They can have the salespeople at each location fax or e-mail the design and quote to the purchasing department, who then processes the paperwork.

There is a caveat to centralized purchasing—quality control. Cabinet dealers produce a lot of paperwork and sometimes that paperwork contains a lot of errors. A salesperson placing their own orders can easily hide their mistakes (and the cost of those mistakes) with a few quick calls to the manufacturer.

Salespeople who also place orders can easily forget items that directly deal with the manufacturer and mark these items as a "service." A centralized purchasing system can easily identify these errors and charge it to the job instead. Initially this can be painful to the sales rep's commissions; however, it teaches the salesperson to be more careful and helps the dealer recapture lost profits.

Industry leaders feel that the best practice is to eliminate all the passing of paper between sales, purchasing, receiving, and accounting by automating the entire process. Dealerships that have made this leap have seen a single purchasing agent be capable of supporting over fifteen salespeople who sell over $30 million worth of kitchens and related products per year.

Should you centralize purchasing? I don't know. But I do know that you should spend a day watching your salespeople. Are they spending the majority of their time doing the things that make a difference in your business? If you answered no, centralizing purchasing can likely be your first step in a more efficient direction.

5

Selling Like a Fox

2009/1/6 Why do some people quote product at very low or no margin? Are they dumb, crazy, or crazy like a fox? I am sure that some are dumb, others are crazy, but what I think we all should focus on is learning from the few who are crazy like a fox.

These are the creative business people who offer an irresistible deal to capture a low profit sale and rely on their selling skills to build back-end profit to the deal.

These business people have discovered that training the sales force to offer specific cross-sell and up-sell opportunities consistently turns marginally profitable customers into profitable ones. If the salesperson can up-sell a marginally profitable customer into a high-margin custom molding or cross-sell into a very profitable lighting system for the glass front cabinets, great margins can be made.

The first step to successful cross and up-selling starts with listening to the customer. Before a highly trained salesperson (a.k.a. sales pro) starts talking about budget, they ask the customer about their wish list and listen carefully to which items they like and which ones they love. Then they quick quote them based on their wish list and ask them how that price compares to their budget. Most of the time, customers are surprised by how much it actually costs to get what they truly want.

The sales pro begins by setting the groundwork for future sales and talks to them about the products that can be removed from the bid but can be purchased later. Then they stress the value of factory-installed upgrades, like dovetail drawer guides.

The key to this successful approach is this: the sales pro lets the low-margin customer know that it is them (the customer) who is in control of how much they spend. The sales pro is simply there to help the customer make educated choices. That's because the sales pro knows that the average kitchen buyer happily extends their budget by approximately 15 percent by investing in upgrades and additional options they learned about during the sales process. In fact, industry research shows the average buyer's main frustration with their salesperson is that the salesperson did not offer them enough upgrade opportunities. Instead of buyer's remorse, customers have remorse that they didn't spend enough!

The key is the sales pro's pressure free, educational approach to sales. They let the prospect know that they are a very valuable resource to them during this process, and they take time to show their product knowledge. They ask their prospects to experience the upgrades. They encourage prospects to have fun and enjoy the process of creating a dream kitchen. They make the prospect feel comfortable enough to ask any question. That's because the more informed the prospect, the more comfortable he/she is in making a big decision.

This is also a critical time for the sales pro to reestablish their company vs. the competition. That's because the sales pro assumes that no matter what the prospect tells them, there are at least two other competitors bidding on the business.

As they are educating the prospect on getting the most kitchen out of their budget, the sales pro also stresses the features and products that cannot be obtained from the competition. That means they take time to shop the competition to understand their offerings. This helps them know how to position themselves as the best alternative. Is their advantage quality? Service? Product? They make sure the prospect knows how to distinguish them before he/she leaves the building.

Beginning salespeople sometimes fall into the rut of describing products and their company's unique value in a very factual manner. The pros know that prospects remember stories and buy based on emotion. So they tell them stories of people who made similar upgrade choices and the benefits they received. They talk about the satisfied customer's emotions. How happy they are. That's because this is more persuasive and memorable to the prospect.

A good open dialogue will offer an attentive salesperson many up-sell and cross-sell opportunities. But it is also important to be attentive to the prospects state of mind. Are they getting tired? Confused? Anxious to make a decision? Sales pros sense this and will stop cross and up-selling so they can ask for the business and close the deal.

They also take time to tell the prospect how much they enjoyed helping them make the right decisions and that they now look forward to helping them get their project underway.

6

Cabinet Salespeople Beware: Designing Isn't Selling

2009/1/22 Cabinet and related product sales is all about the design, isn't it? Or is it?

How is a person going to make such a big investment if they don't have a clear idea of what the kitchen is going to look like after renovation? Yes, design is important; however, should it play such a central role in the process of selling cabinets? Isn't there a better way?

Over the years, I have observed many successful and unsuccessful kitchen cabinet salespeople. I have noticed that those salespeople who struggle in this business make three common mistakes and that those who succeed commonly use two unusual sales techniques. These five items have one thing in common—how design is used during the sales process.

Mistake #1 – Letting Design Drive the Sales Process

Many struggling salespeople see the design as the beginning, middle, and end of their sales efforts. Before getting to know the prospect, their unique needs and desires…the salesperson suggests that they put together a few ideas in a design. These are often the same salespeople who "defend" this design to the prospect instead of listening to them and finding out what they want to buy.

At CompanionCabinet, we suggest using the 4M Sales Process™. The steps are Meet, Measure, Match, and Make the Deal. Under this process, the salesperson may spend two to four hours with the prospect before ever beginning the design process. The focus is on listening and gathering enough information to be able to understand the prospect's needs, and then coming up with a design the prospect loves. This process rests on the knowledge that the more time a prospect invests with a salesperson, and the more the salesperson understands the prospect's views, the more likely the prospect is to buy from that salesperson.

Mistake #2 – Depending on Design Software as a Primary Pricing Tool

Today's popular design software does have the ability to price out kitchen cabinets, depending on the accuracy of the manufacturer's catalog. The problem is countertops, hardware, fixtures, and other common accessories that can't be priced out with design software.

This "pricing gap" leads to a lot of error prone hand calculation and paperwork. The more successful companies either put together computer spreadsheets for pricing or invest in software that provides them with a quoting engine that prices complete jobs accurately, at management-controlled margins.

Mistake #3 –Too Many Redesigns

Some salespeople feel the need to hurry to the design process after learning "just enough" from the prospect to showcase their design skills. This typically results in a "trial and error" approach to sales, leading to many rounds of time-consuming revisions, a poor design, and mutual frustration.

The salesperson should realize that their job is to lead the prospect confidently toward investing in the kitchen of their dreams. To do this the salesperson must listen enough to understand what the prospect wants, the relative priority of those desires, and the budget. With these factors, the salesperson can do "side calculations" to show the cost of an island, different door styles, or an addition of a trash cabinet without having to redesign the entire kitchen. This saves time, effort, and frustration.

The really successful salespeople do a better job of understanding when to design and when to listen. They understand the customer's wants, needs, initial selections, and requirements before they even begin thinking about a design. They then focus on the budget and overall project complexity so that they can recommend the manufacturers and vendors who can meet their prospect's project requirements. They hold themselves to a higher standard of product knowledge and salesmanship.

Of course, there are plenty of other mistakes we could address, but let's move on to some things the most successful cabinet salespeople concentrate on.

Success Standard #1 – No Design Revisits

The pros spend a lot of time understanding the different sales possibilities and upgrade paths that are of interest to the prospect. They carefully assemble a design that gives them the flexibility to show the prospect how the different design components and upgrades can be added or deleted from the basic design. As they present their design to the prospect, they take notes about the prospects ideas and preferences. When they are done, they simply update the design with the prospect's choices and present them with a final design, which brings us to...

Success Standard #2 – Close the Sale When Reviewing the Design

The successful salesperson uses a design review as an opportunity to close the sale. If the person likes what they see, told you what changes they wanted, and agreed that there were no other issues, why shouldn't they buy right then? The only reason for them to look elsewhere is to feel confident that they have considered all of the possibilities.

Sales pros often acknowledge and capitalize on this need by presenting a prospect with three unique designs that match their needs. The prospect then feels like they have considered multiple options and are making the right choice based upon their budget and upgrade preferences, so they are not afraid to commit.

The key to the successful use of design in the cabinet sales effort is timing. If the design is used at the right time and in the right way, it can be a powerful tool for closing a sale. But if it is used too early, or as the backbone of developing a quote, the design can turn into the cause of much wasted time and costly mistakes.

Conclusion

Prospects can tell the difference between the two types of salespeople. The ones that will win the sales are the ones that make it an easy, smooth process to buy cabinets. Following success standards like the ones outlined above is the first step toward making the sale a natural finish to your sales process.

7

2009 Cabinet Dealer Survival Guide

2009/2/18 The other day I was watching TV with my family when a show came on where they dropped this guy in the middle of the desert with little more than a smile. His goal was to survive. It was fascinating watching him use years of British Special Forces training to skillfully navigate through the desert to safety. I would have needed a guide to help me—which is why I thought of writing this article for you.

My family has been in the cabinet industry for over fifty years and survived some pretty harsh conditions. Our industry is facing some pretty harsh conditions now and no expert sees the business getting better in the next four months—and most think it won't get better in 2009.

When they dropped this guy in the desert, he was pre-occupied with water—the way you should be pre-occupied with cash. He did anything he could do to build his store of water.

In 2009, instead of planning for the next six months, companies should assume a twelve-month horizon with little recovery of the market. They need to take actions that will reduce their use of cash and only count on small increases in revenue. Following are six steps cabinet dealers should take immediately, if they don't see their current cash getting them through the next twelve months.

Step #1 – Restructure Employees

No one likes to let go of employees. It is hard to find good ones, and laying them off feels like such a waste. Listen to me. Consolidate duties, lay people off, and make sure everyone is busy. You can't afford to give everyone a semi-vacation until the economy comes back. You should even look at the employees who got a little "over-paid" during the boom time and re-negotiate their salaries in exchange for keeping them employed. Use this rule: Your people should be as busy now as they were two years ago. If you have the right number, it will happen.

Step #2 – Re-negotiate

I mean re-negotiate everything. Talk to your cabinet suppliers, property management, utility companies, and bank. Everyone is open to re-negotiate right now. No supplier wants to either lose a customer or risk not getting paid. Tell your vendors you need lower prices and better payment terms. All of them will listen and many of them will give it to you if you only ask.

Step #3 – Get Rid of "Non-Core" Overhead

What does that mean? Well remember when times were good and you started fabricating counter tops? It was a good idea at the time. It might not be a good idea anymore. That additional overhead is what sucks cash out of your bank account when times are lean. Get out of "non-core" businesses and focus on your strength, distributing cabinets, and use quality third parties to do the other.

Step #4 – Consolidate

Consolidate is just a fancy way of saying get rid of everything you are not using. Sublease warehouse space. Sell trucks you're not using. Review all your equipment and sell anything you are not using, and close any locations that lose more money being open than if they were closed.

Step #5 – Partnerships

In lean times, partnerships can help you reduce cost and increase sales without huge sums of cash. Look at all the people you are currently working with and see if you can suggest a relationship that might help both of you reduce costs. It might be sharing a showroom, warehouse, or delivery staff. Be creative. Maybe approach a flooring or plumbing company to share office space. There are many companies in related industries in the same boat. Figure out how to help each other.

Step #6 – Plan for Cash

Just like the guy in the TV show planning never to run out of water, you have to plan how you'll never run out of cash. In the show, the survival expert had dozens of little tricks to find new sources of water. Friends and family are always challenging, but a likely source of cash. Asking people you know and trust if they know someone who might lend or invest in your company is always a good undertaking. Finding an investor is a very slow process so start now.

Conclusion

Survival in 2009 will be about managing your cash. Take the right steps now to reduce costs, increase revenue, and find new sources of capital. The year 2009 will likely be considered the deep winter of our current recession. By acting on these six steps now, you can ensure you're around to enjoy the beautiful spring that is just around the corner.

CompanionCabinet Software

8

Get "Dressed for the Party"

2009/3/17 The current outlook is grim. All the numbers are discouraging. You might wonder if the market will show ANY signs of "coming back" during all of 2009. Well, as the old saying goes, "every dark cloud has a silver lining," right?

Here's why I believe that.

We Are a Resilient Country

Have you ever noticed that as time goes by, we, as a country, get better at handling crises? It seems like the more we have, the better we get, and the faster we recover. We have more resources to draw from to affect the speed of recovery. This time it goes well beyond our borders. There hasn't been a concerted effort on a global scale to fix something like this since the last world war. Every major developing country is in the crisis together, and all of them are working to make a faster recovery. With that kind of focus, recovery can come faster than any time before, and I believe this one will be surprising (at least for us).

So what does it all mean for dealers over the coming months? And what should we be doing about it?

Be Dressed for the Party

I used to have a recurring dream years ago. I would dream that I was out in the back yard working, getting dirty and sweaty. Then, when finishing my work, I would come into the house and find a house full of people all dressed up for a formal party. Then I would realize I had a large, high profile party at my house that I forgot about and the party was happening right now. I had a house full of people, and my number one goal became how to sneak upstairs so I could get cleaned up and dressed before anyone saw me. That's when I woke up with the horrible feeling that I wasn't ready for my own important party. And worse, I was going to miss a bunch more of it because I had to go get ready.

I look at the current market like my dream.

The Party: We know the market is going to come back. It always does. That's "the party."

Yard Work: The work I was doing in the back yard is what each dealer is doing now to survive the downturn. It's the necessary stuff.

Getting Cleaned Up and Dressed: The "getting cleaned up and dressed for the party" are all those things the dealer has to have in place if they are going to take advantage of the market when it bounces. If the dealer does not do these things, he/she will be scrambling around trying to get "cleaned up and dressed," like I was in my dream, while their competitors are enjoying the party and stealing the majority of the business.

So the question for dealers is, "Will you be dressed and ready when the party arrives?"

How Do I Get Ready for the Party?

Here are five things that I consider necessary "getting dressed" items, so you'll be ready for the party when it happens.

1) Plan Your Infrastructure and Personnel Bounce Back

You've downsized your people and your infrastructure since the market downturn. Many of you are running on 25 to 75 percent capacity of what you had. Many people have left the industry after being let go. Here's the fact: When the market comes back, and demand for your products comes back, all remaining dealers will be trying to hire back the capacity that was let go.

What makes it more important is that so many dealers have gone out of business. So on a market comeback, there is less supply (number of dealers) for the demand. This is GREAT news if you're ready! You may be thinking, "We did it once already when we grew so much up to 2007." But keep in mind, you grew your capacity over years of consistent increase in demand. On an upswing of new demand, be careful you don't just assume you can find all the resources you need on a moment's notice.

When the market comes back this time, you'll have to be much faster to win.

2) Do Your Market Research

Do you have any idea what parts of your market will come back first, and the strongest? Well, you'd better. Those that are watching local trends, forecasts, and keeping track of (and relationships with) all the strong players in each segment will have the advantage when it returns. This is because they'll know right where to go while the others are still trying to figure out what's happening.

3) Get Ready with Third Party Relationships

You should have a plan in place with all third parties you rely upon in your market. You should know THEIR health, and how they will be able to bounce back and pick up capacity. Otherwise, their weakness will put your strength in jeopardy. If there is a possibility for any kind of merger that would make your dealership stronger in the bounce back, now's the time to look at it (it's cheap and you're not too busy to take it on).

4) Be Equally Divided

If there's one lesson everyone has learned this time, it's how hard one part of the market can fall. Many builder-focused dealers in some parts of the country are gone. Many equally divided dealers are still here because they were not solely focused on builders. This is the time to get expertise and capabilities on all sides (builder, retail, multi-family/commercial).

5) Ensure Your Systems and Processes are in Place and Efficient

If you rely on paper and unstructured processes in your business, you'll flounder while others pass you by. Every minute your people spend in manual processes is a minute your good competitors are winning your business. And again, there's no less expensive or more opportune time to get all those things in place than now.

Being in the process and software business, it's amazing how many times I have heard owners say, "We are so busy, we don't have time to slow down and improve our process."

It's the reason one owner said so profoundly, "I love my business, but I hate my job." Dealers should tackle this one now, before they grow again, so that the growth will be more enjoyable and profitable.

We've all seen the parties where certain people seem to be on top of it all, and they enjoy the entire experience at the party. They get to talk to everyone. They build many relationships.

Then there are those that come in late and wonder what they missed. While the people who are dressed for the party make significant inroads and execute on their strategy, these people flounder randomly with no real plan, stumbling into opportunities now and then out of dumb luck. Then they go home and complain about how bad the party was and how they can't seem to figure out how others found it so rewarding.

So don't miss your own, most important party. And even if you do make the party, don't show up all sweaty and grimy—trust me, people won't want to do business with you. But if you take the time NOW to put all these things in place, you'll be in a position not only to enjoy the recovery fully, but also to put your dealership in a top position for years after it.

Now that's a party.

9

How to Make the Most of Consumer Tradeshows

2009/4/15 I love my job! Every day successful cabinet dealers share with me how they accomplish their impressive results, and I get to share this knowledge with you. Recently, I've been curious about the most cost effective manner of generating new leads and I've been surprised at how consistently I get the same answer. Anyone interested in selling more kitchens should read on.

Where to Find Sales Leads

My question for the past several months is, "What is your best source of sales leads?" For many dealers, the most popular answer is, "consumer kitchen and bath shows." The good news is most cities have a large kitchen and bath show; the bad news is these shows require large upfront investments.

If you make the investment, you want to make sure you get the sales. Trade show success seems easy, but generating great booth traffic, qualifying prospects quickly and following up after the show is a challenge. Over the years, I've learned a few tricks that I want to share with you now.

How to Discount Effectively

First, you have to remember that great show traffic doesn't automatically turn into strong booth traffic. There must be a compelling reason for consumers to walk into your booth. My favorite is a prize drawing. The prize should be a large discount, expressed in dollars, off a kitchen remodeling job. I generally suggest a discount that equals the gross margin of your average kitchen sale. This number will be large enough to catch consumers' eyes, motivate them walk in your booth, and fill out an entry form—which gives you the information you need to follow-up with them later.

Shows are all about capturing names. I was always suspicious of the quality of leads generated by a drawing at a show. However, I've learned that consumers don't spend time in booths that showcase products they aren't interested in. So the goal of the prize drawing is to attract the attention of everyone interested in a kitchen remodel and compel them to identify themselves as prospects by taking the time and making the effort to fill out the entry form—and trusting that those who could care less about kitchen remodeling will not waste their time by walking in your booth.

How you handle the people who choose to enter your booth will determine how successful the show is at generating quick sales. Prospects are not created equal. Some prospects are ready to buy now and others won't be ready until years from now. Your booth personnel must be able to tell the difference quickly.

Qualifying Early

If your staff asks each consumer, "Do you have a brand and style of cabinet that you're particularly interested in?" The consumer's response will tell them everything that they need to know. Most consumers who are close to buying have already developed a preference for specific brands and products.

If the person tells you a brand and style, they are in the final stages of their decision process. They have considered remodeling their kitchen, educated themselves on the products and brands, and formed an opinion on which product will meet their needs best. These prospects need a salesperson that can help them understand how to turn their vision into reality.

Marketing to Hot Prospects

Two marketing techniques are very effective with these prospects. First, give "hot" prospects special collateral materials that clearly enumerate the reasons why they should choose to do business with your dealership, rather than anyplace else. Be specific. Is it quality, breadth of products, service, price, or something else? Give specific examples of how you deliver this unusual value.

The material should also contain a personal profile of the designer with whom they will be working. The profile should describe the designer's remodeling experience and qualifications. The goal is to give the prospect material that makes them comfortable that both the designer and company are extremely skilled and accomplished professionals.

Meet the Owner

The purpose of the second technique is to make their visit to your booth **memorable**. The prospect needs to meet the owner of the company. What the owner says is critical. The owner needs to look the prospect in the eye and tell them how much they appreciated them coming into the booth, and then tell them why they should buy a kitchen from them (Price, quality, service, etc.), and then express a clear desire to do whatever it takes to do business with them.

Everyone likes to do business with a company where they know the owner, and meeting an owner so interested in them is memorable. Use this fact to your advantage.

Marketing to Early-Stage Prospects

What do you do with the prospects that don't have a brand in mind? Give them different collateral materials. These materials should be more educational in nature. The information should help the prospect be able to understand the major products, how they differ in quality, and their approximate cost. You want to help them get to the point where they feel knowledgeable enough to make an informed choice. This could take weeks, months, or even years.

Your goal with these prospects is to position yourself as the expert source of information they need to figure out their remodeling project. You can gain their loyalty and shape their buying preferences by educating them on the critical factors they need to consider when making their decision and impressing them with your insights, knowledge, and listening skills.

How to cost effectively cultivate these warm leads into hot prospects is a topic I'll cover in a future article. But until then, heed the advice I shared with you today. The last person who followed these suggestions reported back that they generated 135 quality leads in a single weekend—more than twice the number of leads they had generated in the past.

10

How Are You Unique?

2009/5/5 "Why should I buy from you?" said the prospect to the anxious salesperson. There was an awkward silence, and then the salesperson responded with a lot of conversation about superior service, great staff, and competitive prices. The prospect stared blankly at the salesperson and then turned to his wife and said, "Isn't that what the last place said?" She nodded her head in agreement, then slowly turned and left the showroom. The salesperson turned to the owner and asked, "What should I have said?"

Most cabinet dealers wouldn't really know how to respond. They like to talk about their superior service and years of experience, but that story doesn't seem to play to everyone. And with how tough business is, the owner really just wants to know what to say to get the prospect to buy.

The Real Story

Here is the real story: There is no one thing you can say that will get every prospect to buy from you. There are many different types of people who are all searching for different things from a cabinet dealer. Your challenge is that you can't be all things to all people. You must make a choice about how your business is unique—and that choice will mean that some people will never buy from you. Your goal is to find a way to be unique so that enough prospects will have a preference for doing business with you.

Seven Ways to be Unique

There are many ways that businesses can choose to be unique, but only seven of them are important and valuable to prospects. They are:

- Breadth of Product
- Breadth of Service
- Quality of Product
- Quality of Service
- Price
- Speed
- Guarantee

Just Pick One for Pete's Sake

Being unique means taking one of these seven business characteristics and exceeding the standard that is present in your marketplace. Notice how I said "one," not three, not one and a half, just one. If your competitors all carry three lines of cabinets and countertops, and you choose to be unique based upon your breadth of product, you should have at least eight cabinet lines, multiple grades of countertops, appliances, hardware, and plumbing fixtures. When someone walks into your showroom, he or she should be overwhelmed with the quantity of options available. They should believe that they should do business with you because you have everything they could want in this single location.

Quality is a basis of competition on which many cabinet dealers feel they can compete. Whether it is competing on the quality of a product or service, most business owners make the same mistake—they don't talk specifically about how they provide quality.

It is easy to say that a cabinet is high quality. Shoot, everyone says that. What makes you effective at competing based on quality is how uniquely you can talk about quality. It's not enough to talk about a cabinet as being high quality; you must talk specifically about it and what that means to the prospect. Is the finish richer? Are the shelves thicker? Are the hinges heavier duty? If they are, what does that mean to the consumer?

Speed is an unusual way to compete in the cabinet business, but it can be effective for the right prospect. Competing on speed means that your business can take the order for the kitchen and have it delivered and installed faster than any other business in town. Contractors will sometimes pay slight premiums for getting the kitchen installed quickly. If enough prospects will pay a premium for getting their kitchen installed quickly, then speed is a good way to make your business unique.

A guarantee is given by most cabinet dealers but a cabinet dealer who is competing based upon their guarantee must do something that is "over the top" and memorable. The guarantee might be that any customer who is dissatisfied with any part of their kitchen—no matter what the cause— will get a 50 percent discount. The point of the guarantee is to make the prospect feel as if doing business with the company is irresistible because there is little to lose by choosing the company versus the others.

The Toughest Way to Make Money

The final way to compete is based on price. Competing on price is the easiest way to generate sales and the hardest way to make money. Offering the lowest price attracts prospects, but the dealership can't offer the same quality, service, and guarantee at a radically lower price. They must find and create ways to deliver an acceptable level of quality and service at an impressively low price. This generally translates into a no-frills showroom with inexpensive cabinet construction and low service levels. Many prospects will be attracted by the low prices, but you must figure out how to deliver consistent profits at these low margins.

Conclusion

There is no one way of competing that is always superior to the others. The point is that if you want to be successful, you must choose how you are going to compete and then train **everyone** to tell prospects **specifically** how you deliver on your claim.

11

Big Sale Gone Bad

2009/5/19 I hate situations like this, and I'm starting to hear stories of cabinet dealers facing it more and more frequently. Here's what happens: You work to get a builder's business for years and finally win it. You get a shot at a new sub-division going up. You have some great designs and a sharp pencil. You win the business and do the first couple of houses. Everything is great. Then it happens. Or should I say, it doesn't happen?

The payments that began so promptly are starting to get more and more late with each new house. The builder is happy with your work, other than the microscopic mark in the cabinet door he tells you about, almost trying to justify a late payment because it hasn't been touched up yet. It seems like a difficult topic and you need the business, so why say anything?

After a while, you start having some cash flow challenges and look at a list of people who owe you money. This is the first time you realize your coveted builder owes you over

$75,000. What do you do now? What should you have done before?

What I want to share with you are a couple of ideas that should help you if you are facing this situation now, and help you avoid it in the future.

Step One

In the previous market, many were scared to ask builders for too much information. We were just "lucky to get the business." Those days are gone. Now you need to have a standard "new customer" packet that you have **all** new customers complete. Ask for detailed financial information including major creditors, names of banks and bank account numbers, and a release allowing you to confirm the information is accurate. The credit application should also include a provision that in the event a lawsuit is required to collect any debt, the creditor will also be able to collect legal fees and the cost of collection. It is also good practice to ask for a personal guarantee, depending on the size of the company. A credit application with their credit policies and trade terms documented will help you tremendously if trouble occurs later.

CompanionCabinet Software

Step Two

Begin your collection process early. If your invoice is due in thirty days, have an administrative person place a pleasant call to your builders accounts payable department and inquire about when your invoice is scheduled for payment. If the check has already been issued, great. If not, you'll either have a date the check will be cut or a clear indication that your check is being held. Either piece of information is better to know now rather than later.

A receivable is just like a perishable fruit. It's most valuable when you get it on its due date. The older it gets, the less its worth. A little known fact is the "secret of sixty." The secret of sixty is that the more a receivable gets past sixty days, the more unlikely it is that you will ever collect it. The truth is that once a builder falls behind in payments, they generally fall further behind until someone is never paid. Your goal is to make sure that you always get paid.

Step Three

Once the invoice is thirty days past due, send a letter with a firm tone asking for the invoice to be paid. A telephone follow-up call also should occur. The topics of the conversation are that the bill is past due and that you would like to receive payment. If required, explain that you have a strict collections policy and that you refer people to collections when they are sixty days past due.

Step Four

When a person reaches sixty days past due, send them a demand letter. A demand letter indicates a deadline for payment and the total amount due. Ask for them to contact you if they cannot immediately pay the debt and you will arrange a payment plan. The letter should also state that legal action will be taken to collect the debt if it is not received by the due date.

Step Five

Always have payment plans in writing. It is easy to be in agreement on the phone but in disagreement in the future when a check is due and you and the builder remember differently. This is probably the biggest point of frustration in business. You feel like you did everything right, were patient and you still can't win. Write down the installment plan in the form of a memo, send it to the builder, and hold the builder to it.

Step Six

At sixty days past due, have your attorney send the builder a letter. Review the desired payment time line and amount due, and state that you will take legal action to collect the debt. Also indicate that this letter is the final warning before a lawsuit is filed and that no further letters will be sent.

Step Seven

File a lawsuit. Depending on the amount of the debt and the state in which you live, you can either file a claim in superior court or small claims court. Small claims court filing fees are low, attorneys are not allowed, and the disputes are settled within a couple of months. One challenge of small claims court is that a creditor (you in this case) cannot appeal the decision. With that fact in mind, be prepared to choose the small claims court route.

Superior court will only make sense for larger debts. The debtor is served with a court summons and complaint and will have thirty days to file an answer. Unless the builder contests the validity of the debt, most collection claims proceed quickly either to settlement or judgment.

Conclusion

Remember the phrase "the squeaky wheel gets the grease"? Well, this is the time you want to be the squeaky wheel. It's your money at stake. Most builders will pay you rather than endure this process. It creates stress and hassles for them and they will most likely decide it is easier to pay you rather than live through all these hassles—especially when their other creditors aren't following this process.

A common question I always get is, "Doesn't this scare some business away?"

And I always answer the same way: "Why yes it does. It scares off the kind of business you never wanted anyway!"

CompanionCabinet Software

12

New Breed of Manufacturer Reps Emerging... Finally

2009/6/2 In this industry, manufacturer reps have historically been solely focused on selling their product line. Their time is spent signing up new dealers to sell their product, and most of their efforts and conversation are centered on convincing dealers to begin selling their line (or to continue selling their line).

Even with that limited scope, many reps don't even have an in-depth knowledge of their own line. They know the selling points, but it doesn't go much deeper than that. Well, this type of rep doesn't have much value in today's market.

The New World of Reps

Let me describe to you the new world of manufacturer reps that are emerging.

Manufacturer reps typically have limited territories where they spend their time. They know all of the major players in their territory, and they know a lot about those major players. These reps travel their territory frequently and meet with as many key people as they can (and not just dealers). They are exposed to so much information as they travel and make their connections that they are in a unique position of knowledge about their markets, more so than any dealer could be. It's a matter of exposure to all the "goings on" in a market that dealers can't keep up with.

The interesting thing is that when the reps visit dealers, they're not there pitching their product. They are there having a valuable conversation about what's happening with the dealer (or other businesses), teaching them what they know, and helping them improve by the knowledge they share with them. The formal "sales pitch" to the dealer almost becomes unnecessary. As a bi-product of a good relationship, the dealer will discover what the rep sells.

Below are some of the key capabilities of these reps:
1. **They know their markets** – They keep up with, and know what's going on in their markets. They know what trends are emerging in each of their markets and the effect of those trends on dealers. They study the large companies that drive demand in their markets and know what they're up to and how it will affect the dealers in the

area. They have an in-depth knowledge of what is working and not working in their markets, as well as what's coming.

2. **They know the manufacturer landscape** – They have a comprehensive knowledge of all the major manufacturers that sell in their markets. Some of them are more informed about a manufacturer than the manufacturer's own rep is.

3. **They have a broad network** – They have valuable connections with many manufacturers, their reps, many dealers, many local suppliers, salespeople, business people, and others. They have spent years building this network so that they have multiple points to make a connection with dealers and others.

4. **They have been in the dealer business** – Many of these great reps have a background in the industry. They have owned businesses, run businesses, been salespeople, and so on. Because of this, they have a perspective that stands above the rest, in that they understand the unique problems of the dealers. If there's one thing dealers recognize quickly, it's whether someone trying to sell them something has been in their shoes or not.

5. **They know dealer operations** – Because of their research and experience in the industry, and from their relationships with so many different dealers,

they have a deep level of knowledge of how a dealership should run effectively (or they have specific areas of targeted expertise). As a result, they can provide great value to a dealer as they observe the dealer function, and recommend improvements along the way. They can help dealers with anything from a better organizational structure, to the type of software they should be using, to how best to negotiate with their suppliers, and much more. This kind of interaction is the most effective in winning the dealer's trust for a long time.

Why is This Valuable?

So why are these reps so valuable when you find one? It's because they are almost like industry consultants. They have huge knowledge value that dealers need, but dealers are too busy running their business to spend the time needed to gain it themselves. They would have to pay someone else to coach them. And the best thing is, these reps don't charge for the coaching. They know that by helping the dealer succeed, the business will eventually come their way to stay. So they look at it as an investment.

Here are some examples of the specific challenges ALL reps should be able to help dealers with:

- What kind of marketing is working best in my market, and is it worth the expense?
- Should I take on this new related product line to bring in more revenue?
- Are there any companies or individuals looking to buy dealers in my market?
- Is there any software that could revitalize the way I do business?
- What's going on in my market that I should be concerned with, or aware of?
- What is my competition doing, and how well are they doing it?
- Where can I find some good salespeople?
- What's a better structure for my business as far as employees are concerned?
- What should I be inventorying, if anything?

If reps can talk intelligently about these things and "coach" dealers in ways where dealers end up saying "I wish I could hire... (Joe rep)," then that rep is going to be invaluable to the dealer. If a rep can't talk intelligently about these things, then it's just wasting time (the reps' and the dealers').

Where Are These Reps?

So where do we find these reps? Well, that's a tricky question. But here are some clues:

Manufacturer rep organization – It's rare to find these reps working as an "employee" for most manufacturers. These reps are the "movers and shakers" in the industry. They aren't usually satisfied simply working as an employee. If they are working as an employee, then the manufacturer has succeeded in creating a very entrepreneurial environment. These reps want to shake things up and pave new ground.

One question to rule them all – If a rep walks in your door, here's the one question to find out his worth in a matter of a few minutes: "Tell me what's happening in my market." He should be able to impress the heck out of you with his grasp of what's happening that you didn't even know about. That's a clear sign you're dealing with a keeper.

Summary

The old paradigm of being a manufacturer's rep is slowly going away. They are being replaced by a valuable new breed of reps that have an entirely different focus.

The difference between the new breed of manufacturer reps and the "old model" reps comes down to this: Dealers look forward to visits from the new breed, and they want to avoid the interruption of visits from the old. Why? Because they are actually getting business value from the good reps every time they meet. It's not a sales meeting; it's a coaching session. These reps know that coaching sessions naturally turn into sales meetings once the trust is built.

13

How to Stay Up When Sales are Down

2009/6/20 The other day I ran a "googledex" analysis on the economy. I use "googledex" as a term for when I enter a topic into Google and gauge mood on a topic by reviewing the titles on the first three result pages. It isn't scientific but it's really interesting.

When I typed in "economy," twenty-three titles were on the first three pages. Five titles were hopeful, three neutral, and fifteen negative. That made a three to one negative "googledex." No wonder everyone is depressed about our economy and worried about their jobs. The mood about the economy is very negative.

Don't get me wrong; with the economy being as it is, I believe we all have more than enough of a reason to feel down. But that brings up an interesting issue. How many prospects yearn to buy from a sad salesperson? Doom and gloom doesn't really inspire confidence now does it? So if you are feeling down, but your sales need to go up, what are you to do?

I take my cue from Viktor Frankl. Viktor said, "The last of the human freedoms, to choose one's attitude in any given set of circumstances, is to choose ones way." Viktor Frankl was a psychologist and holocaust survivor who noticed that the choice of attitude among concentration camp prisoners influenced their fate.

Prisoners who chose to give into the hopelessness of their situation seemed to perish quickly and those who chose to be positive managed better. People, who choose to be positive, no matter what their circumstances, fare better than those who do not. The same is especially true of salespeople.

So if you are feeling a little down, here are ten tips to help you choose to have a more positive attitude:

1. Take 100 Percent Responsibility – When you are 100 percent responsible for your results, you are 100 percent in control of your future. Being in control makes humans happy. It is that simple.

2. Don't Take "No" Personally – If you question yourself every time you hear a "No" in sales, you'll question yourself often and be unhappy forever.

3. Set Goals – People feel happier when they are progressing toward a destination; however, with no goals, there is no destination or feeling of progress.

4. Manage and Organize Your Time – Working hard but making no progress is depressing, but working smart and achieving goals makes you feel happy.

5. See Obstacles as Challenges, Not Excuses – An obstacle can be seen as a reason to quit or an opportunity to grow. Quitting makes us sad and growing makes us happy.

6. Don't Talk about Downbeat Topics – There is an old saying, "What we talk about is what we are." If you talk about negative topics, you become a negative person.

7. Stop Complaining – Complain to someone who can do something about your issue once and let it go. You have goals to achieve and challenges to overcome, so don't waste your time complaining about things that aren't going to change to people who can't do anything about it.

8. Avoid Saying, "You're Wrong" – I can't remember the last time I witnessed a positive conversation that began with "you're wrong." Can you?

9. Avoid Saying, "But" – "But" is used in conversations to transition from insincere thoughts to honest ones. For example, "I think you have the best product, but I want to go in another direction." Just say what you think and people will respect you.

10. Avoid Saying Negative Things – Do I need to say more? I've never heard someone say, "I just love to be around him, he's so negative."

In closing, let me give you a bonus thought. The attitude you convey is driven by the meaning you choose to place on the events that occur in your life. If you lose a sale, you can choose to believe that it means you're a bad salesperson and become depressed, or you can choose to believe that sales is a numbers game and that a "no" is a good thing because it moves you one step closer to someone who will say "yes." Same event, but vastly different attitudes.

Now go forth and be happy!

14

The First Impression

2009/7/8 Put yourself in the prospects' shoes. They have a big decision to make. Should they spend a small fortune remodeling their kitchen or just sit tight?

On one hand, they are excited about how attractive an updated kitchen will be, but on the other hand, they fear how much time and money it will take. They've done their research. They are walking in your showroom because they think you might have something they want and they want to see if they can find it.

As you approach them, you make eye contact with one another. A small smile breaks across each of your faces, sort of an acknowledgement that you are about to speak to each other. As you approach them, a million things are running through your mind, most of them having to do with jobs you're already working on.

Put Yourself in Their Shoes

You greet one another and the prospect tells you they are only looking. But what do you think the prospect is really thinking?

I know. They're thinking:
- "What is he going to try to sell me?"
- "Why should I trust him?"
- "How much is this going to cost?"

Most prospects assume salespeople are going to be of little to no value to them.

If you are in sales, you have about three seconds to turn this unfavorable assumption about you into a favorable impression. Those first three seconds sets the stage for the rest of your relationship with the prospect. The impression you make in this first meeting will determine if you are treated as a servant, who calculates prices and creates design, or as a trusted advisor, who helps them make a big decision.

How do you become a trusted advisor? What do you say? What is the difference between success and failure? Focus. First, you have to shut everything else out of your mind and make that prospect the most important thing in your world.

Then follow this process:

1. Make a Social Connection

People buy from people, and your first order of business is to let this new prospect know that you are the type of person they would feel comfortable doing business with. Work to get a conversation going. Ask what brought them into the store today or to comment on a neat new product that is in your showroom. The point is that you want them to share some information with you so you can show them that you listen to what they say.

2. Find Some Common Social Ground

Ask about where they live, their family, or recreational activities that they enjoy. You want to find a social topic that you can share with the prospect. Being able to talk about a common interest with the prospect subtly says, "I am just like you and you can trust me."

3. Let the Prospect Set the Pace

If they want to move to business quickly, don't frustrate them by talking endlessly about your trip to Florida. Ask questions to understand what they want. Don't just try to understand the products they want, but try to understand why they want them. After you think you understand their situation, you should repeat it back to them. When you do, they will think to themselves, "He understands me and can help me find what I want." I cannot stress enough how showing you listen well creates a favorable impression.

4. Share a Little about Yourself

Tell a short story about how you helped a person in a very similar situation to theirs. Tell about the frustrations the customer had and how you helped them find a solution, how the solution was delivered, and how much the customer enjoyed it. Tell details and make the story vivid. This will get your new prospect thinking, "I need to listen to this person because he/she can help me make a good decision."

5. Talk a Little about Your Company

Tell specifically how your company can deliver something uniquely valuable to this prospect. You can talk about service, quality, one-stop shopping, or fast delivery, but you must be specific. "We have great service" means nothing, but talking about a company policy that ensures all service calls are returned within four hours and all problems are addressed within twenty-four hours means everything.

Soon the prospect is thinking that this dealership offers him something uniquely valuable for his money.

Summary

This series of steps quickly turns the prospects negative assumptions about a salesperson into a positive impression of you. You have set the stage to ask detailed questions about their project, time frames, budget, and other dealerships they have visited in a stress free manner. As an advisor, these are all legitimate questions you need answered to make excellent recommendations.

By following these few simple techniques, you have set the stage for winning the sale. You have taken yourself from being in a poor selling position to a position of influence. As a trusted advisor, you guide a prospect smoothly to a decision on what to buy and from whom. The key is using the relationship you established in this first meeting to guide them to making a decision while allowing the prospect to feel like they are always in control.

Keeping this balance is tricky, and in my next article, I'll give you some tips on how to accomplish it.

15

Economic Drought Hits Cabinet Industry – Catfish Hold Secret to Survival

2009/7/23 What can catfish teach cabinet dealers about today's economy? A lot! These fish frequently deal with droughts and have two survival strategies that are perfect models for cabinet dealers who are dealing with this economic drought. Catfish either skedaddle or hunker down. When you strip everything else away, cabinet dealers only have the same two choices. Let me explain.

How Catfish Survive

In Southeast Asia, there is a breed of catfish called "the walking catfish." The walking catfish lives in rice paddies, ponds, and swamps, the kind of environment that "dries up" when a drought occurs. As the water recedes, there are too many fish trying to survive in too little water.

Does this feel familiar?

Soon, both the quality of the water and quantity of food begin to diminish. Once "the walking catfish" detects its pond is drying up, it does something bold. It gets out of the water and "walks" to a new and more promising pond.

Cabinet dealers can use the same strategy. Many cabinet dealers are already migrating. When business was more plentiful, many dealerships expanded into new "ponds" or communities around them. Today many of these smaller communities no longer have the level of business required to support a satellite office, and prudent dealerships are withdrawing from these small ponds and "walking back" home.

A slightly different version of this same strategy is open to the cabinet dealerships who defined their market as new construction builders. This pond shrank and those dealers who focused on builders needed to migrate to the higher margin remodel market. The remodel pond requires different skills, but the customers will let the dealer work at a profit.

The second catfish strategy is to hunker down. The African lungfish is the perfect example of this. When a drought occurs, the lungfish digs deep into the mud and buries itself. Then the catfish goes into a stupor, stops feeding, and becomes inactive. The cocoon of mud keeps the fish from de-hydrating and their inactivity slows their metabolism. Although they may appear to be in great peril, their chances of survival are good because they are prepared to deal with the harsh conditions. They are in a state that allows them to survive with little food or water. After the drought lifts, the water returns and the lungfish become active.

Cabinet Dealer Survival Strategies

Many dealers have begun adopting the lungfish's survival strategy. These dealerships have trimmed back staff and lowered their economic "metabolism." By lowering their "metabolism" these dealerships survive on less revenue and cash flow. They also "cover up with mud" by trimming the quantity of people they are doing business with and burrowing into their most loyal customers. They "root out" what little cash is left in their shrinking pond of customers. When the drought lifts, these dealerships, like the lungfish, will have survived and be able to return to their former levels of vitality.

No matter what catfish strategy you choose, winning most of the business that you get a crack at will be an important success factor. Three activities are key.

First, you must target your customers. To build your business you need to narrow your focus to a smaller set of customers and prospects and service them well.

Second, review your sales activities and ensure you are "servicing" as well as "selling" your prospects. Servicing is creating designs and responding to prospect's requests. It is a part of getting the prospect to buy, but it is not the most important part. The selling part is what gets the prospect to buy from you rather than the competition. Your salespeople have to sell by:

1. Positioning themselves as experts
2. Positioning your company as the preferred place to do business
3. Getting the prospect to make a buying decision now

And finally, you have to deliver your customer compelling value. Reputation in tough times is everything. The cabinet industry is a cyclical business and when times are good, customers learned to deal with bad service. Now that times are tougher, service must be impeccable. Your customers' experience must be so outstanding that they tell their friends about you. That is called word of mouth advertising; it's free, and it's your key to survival.

Summary

There you have it—a catfish's guide to economic survival. I hope you enjoyed my analogy. Please consider your situation and adopt a strategy. I love this business and I'd love to see you talking about how you survived the drought in years to come.

16

And Now, for the Good News

2009/8/10 For months now, there has been a bombardment of news, both good and bad on the condition of the housing market, as well as speculation as to what's going to happen. Because of the quantity of articles and new stories produced, I decided to try to put the good news history over the last few months together and get a perspective of what the trend really is and make sense of it.

Below is the recent history of the key pieces of news that I believe have led us to a turning point in the housing market.

April 3, 2009 – Radar Logic reported that year-over-year decline in home sales went from (-36 percent) in 2008 to (-06 percent) in 2009. CEO Michael Feder said, *"There appears to be a significant increase in demand given the reduction in prices evident in many markets."*

April 15, 2009 – National Association of Home Builders (NAHB) announced that *builder confidence*, as measured by NAHB/Wells Fargo Housing Market Index (HMI), had its largest one-month increase since May 2003. In response, NAHB Chief Economist David Crowe said, *"This is a very encouraging sign that we are at or near the bottom of the current housing depression."*

April 23, 2009 – Radar Logic's RPX Monthly Housing Market Report for February said that thirteen of the twenty-five metropolitan areas covered by the report posted their largest month-over-month increases for the month of February since 2006. On the same day, the National Association of Realtors (NAR) announced that first-time buyers returned to the housing market in March. NAR Chief Economist Lawrence Yun stated the housing market *"appeared to be stabilizing with modest ups and downs."*

April 28, 2009 – Standard & Poor's released the S&P/ Case-Shiller Home Price Indices (CSI) for February, and David Blitzer, Chairman of Standard & Poor's Index Committees, remarked that *"while the decline in residential real estate continued into February, we witnessed some deceleration in the rate of decline in some of the markets."*

The Indications of Stability Became Stronger in May

May 18, 2009 – NAHB announced that builder confidence increased again in April.

May 21, 2009 – RPX Monthly Housing Market Report for March indicated that after the index had fallen continually throughout 2008, and had been virtually flat in February and March 2009, things are beginning to change. *"While not a bottom, the stability in home prices we are seeing is certainly good news"* (Michael Feder, CEO Radar Logic).

May 27, 2009 – The Federal Housing Finance Agency (FHFA) announced that the pace of decline in its purchase-only home price index had declined considerably. FHFA Director James B. Lockhart said *"Our latest data are consistent with growing evidence that housing market conditions may be stabilizing in some parts of the country."* On the same day, NAR announced that existing home sales rose in April with strong activity in lower price ranges.

June Milestone (Three Months of Stability in the RPX Composite Index)

June 10, 2009 – The RPX Composite Index rose for the third month in a row, and in a Bloomberg TV interview, Michael Feder said *"We are now back at what would have been a logical inflated price for housing given natural forces… perhaps what we'll see over the next several months is a real recovery."*

July 16, 2009 – NAHB announced that builder confidence increased again in July, and David Crowe said, *"The market is bouncing around a bottom."*

July Milestone (Three Months of Consecutive Increases in Home Sales)

July 23, 2009 – NAR announced that existing home sales increased 3.6 percent in May, the third monthly increase in a row. Lawrence Yun, NAR's Chief Economist said *"This is another hopeful sign – if we can keep the volume of sales above the level of new inventory, prices could stabilize in many areas around the end of the year."*

July 23, 2009 – At the release of Radar Logic's monthly report, Michael Feder said, *"At this point we are comfortable with the observation that RPX values in much of the country have bottomed, at least for now."*

July Milestone (Four Months of Consecutive Increases in the Case-Shiller Composite Index)

July 28, 2009 – Standard & Poor's announced that the Case-Shiller composite indices had increased for the fourth consecutive month. David Blitzer said, *"To put it in perspective, this is the first time we have seen broad increased in home prices in 34 months. This could be an indication that home price declines are finally stabilizing."*

The Seasonal Excuse

Some of the good news can be explained by regular seasonal trends that would indicate that April through May increases are to be expected. There are three pieces of good news here:

1. Seasonal strength was largely absent in the spring/summer of 2008, but very apparent in 2009.
2. The increases in 2009 have lasted longer than would be expected by seasonal trends alone.
3. The increases in 2009 are greater than the average of what would be expected considering seasonal trends over the period 2000-2008.

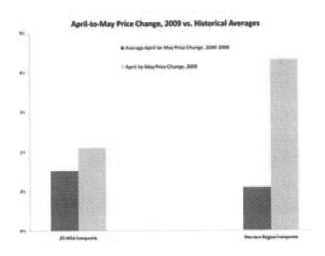

Summary

We are seeing much more consistent good news to indicate that we have hit the bottom of the market recession from a housing market perspective. The big question now is how long will it take to come back to a respectable level?

That's the million-dollar question, but at least now I believe we can somewhat comfortably say, *"The worst is over."*

17

Increasing Sales without Generating More Leads

2009/8/23 I talk with dealers all across the U.S. each day. Many of them are concerned about how their designers will generate more leads. The question is the same, regardless of how big or small you are, how many people you have laid off or hired, or how many designers you have. The question still remains:

How do you generate more revenue when there aren't enough leads to go around?

When I ask these dealers about how they are tackling their sales challenges, the topic of closing rates never seems to come up. It's always discussion of generating more leads, more show room traffic, more word of mouth networking, or more…(fill in the blank here). The focus is always around bringing *more* people in the door.

The Boat Just Left, and You Weren't On It

That's when I realized they're missing the boat.

The topic of closing rates eventually does come up, because I can't wait any longer and I have to ask it. I usually get answers like this:

- "They're pretty good...."
- "Uhmm...I would say...uhmm...(fill in guess here)."
- "I'm not really sure, but our designers have been here a while and they're really good."

Very rarely do I get a closing rate percentage that is actually based on solid measurement. And that's a problem. A very big problem, actually. Not understanding your closing rates means you're guessing. If you're guessing on the revenue-generating arm of your business, that's really dangerous because that means you don't know how many revenue opportunities you're missing.

Generating More Revenue

Generating more revenue for your dealership can come in two ways. First, we can use the "more" concept I mentioned earlier (e.g., finding more leads). But that's one of the hardest ways to tackle the sales challenge in a market like this. It takes time, money which you probably don't have right now, and some seriously creative marketing ideas.

The other way to generate more revenue is much easier. Yet it continues to escape many dealers. And that is to *close more* of what is already coming in the door. In other words, to increase your designer's closing rates.

Some Simple Math

Let's take a simple example. A "prospect" for this discussion is anyone who actually visits your showroom. A "lead" is someone we might market to but hasn't necessarily walked into your dealership yet.

We'll assume the following to keep the math easy:

Avg Job = $10,000
Current Avg. Closing Rates = 30%

If one hundred prospects walk into the showroom, we would expect to close thirty *(100 prospects X 30% closing rate = 30 wins)* sales yielding us $300K in revenue *(30 wins X $10K = $300K)*. Of course you need to get one hundred prospects to walk in your door each month, which means you have to talk to much more than one hundred prospects because many people you talk to won't be interested in checking out the showroom in this market. A common rule of marketing is to apply a factor of ten if you're not sure how many leads you need to get a certain number of prospects to walk in the door. If you want one hundred people in your showroom that month, you should plan on marketing to one thousand potential leads.

This is an overwhelming number for a designer in just one month. Their Rolodex just isn't that big.

A Different Way of Looking at the Problem

Here's another way to look at this problem, which isn't so overwhelming—just increase your designer's closing rates.

Let's assume for a moment we could increase closing rates to 65 percent (I know it sounds crazy, but the high producing designers are doing this and more, so you can too). Now to get our $300K in revenue, the math would like this:

| Avg Job = $10,000 |
| Current Avg. Closing Rates = 65% |

If one hundred prospects walk in the door and we closed sixty-five of them, we would beat our $300K mark by a mile (*100 prospects X 65% closing rates = 65 wins, or $650K in revenue*). So, let's instead stick with our target of $300K

(30 kitchen jobs X $10K = $300K) and figure out how many prospects we would need, because I want to drive home the point that you can do $300K in revenue with a lot less effort than you might think. The math looks like this:

30 jobs / 65% closing rate = 46.15 prospects (walk-ins) needed (we'll round down to 46).

Now we only need forty-six of those same prospects to walk into the showroom to get our $300K in revenue. The problem has just been cut in half, and we didn't even take out a magazine ad yet.

People Who Close More Also Sell Above Average

Designers with higher closing rates are also masters at getting their customers to understand the importance (and benefits) of smart upgrades that stretch the customer's original budget. These designers can grow a typical sale by 25 percent or more by just engendering trust in their relationships and educating consumers at key points in the sales process.

Factoring this in, let's look back at our math example one final time.

Avg Job = $10,000 * 1.25 = $12,500
Current Avg. Closing Rates = 65%

Doing the Same Volume with Less Work

The first thing to notice is now only twenty-four jobs need to close to generate $300K in revenue *($300,000 target revenue / $12,500 avg job)*.

Now we can calculate how many prospects we need to talk to get to twenty-four jobs with our 65 percent closing rates.

24/65% = 36.9 prospects, (we'll round up to 37 for easier math)

Now we only need thirty-seven of those same prospects to walk into the showroom to get our $300K in revenue. I think we can all agree this is much more manageable for a designer.

Summary

Math sometimes gives me a headache too, but below is a summary of it all for easy reference:

CompanionCabinet Software

Example	Avg Job	# Prospects (Walk-ins) Needed	Avg Closing Rate	# Wins Needed	Revenue Generated	# Leads Needed
Low Closing Rate	$10,000	100	30%	30	$300,000	1,000
High Closing Rate	$10,000	46	65%	30	$299,000	460
High Closing Rate & Higher Avg Job	$12,500	37	65%	24	$300,625	370

There are two major lessons to this story:

- Assuming your showroom isn't completely dead, concentrate on increasing your closing rates as the #1 goal for your sales team.
- Make the most of every sale by educating consumers so they will upgrade.

The only way you can do this is to develop an understanding of the closing rates for each of your designers as soon as possible. Once you have this baseline, start implementing a consistent, repeatable sales process that everyone can *easily* follow so you can target areas for improvement.

It's not magic—it's science. Nail the science of sales first; then you can mix in the art of sales later.

18

Use Tax – Your Competitive Advantage or Just More Cash?

2009/9/3 You may have heard about it. You may be doing it. Or maybe it passed you by and you've been entirely missing the opportunity. If so, you have been missing out on potentially a lot of money.

The question is, are you collecting and paying "sales tax" on the cabinets you sell and install? Meaning, are you calculating the tax you charge and paying on the "sales price" of the job, which in many states includes the delivery and installation charge? If so, you're missing out on probably the easiest way to be more competitive and profitable.

Here's the deal

In most states the law provides that a sale of materials, such as cabinets and related products, that are sold and installed to become a component of "real property" (i.e., a house – new OR existing) constitutes what is called a "performance contract" or "capital improvement." A performance contract is where a consumer is paying the dealer or company to provide goods and install them (and they become part of the real property). "Install" being the key ingredient to constitute a performance contract.

Consumers aren't showing up and purchasing retail goods and leaving with them on their truck. They're paying you to complete a portion of their real property with goods and services. This scenario constitutes a performance contract instead of a "retail sale" where you would have to charge "sales tax."

So What?

Well, for a performance contract, you don't collect and pay retail "sales tax" on your full sales price. Retail sales tax is what most dealers are collecting and paying currently, and it is calculated on the total sales price of the goods, including delivery and installation in many states. For a performance contract, you calculate the tax on the "cost" of the goods you purchase to complete the performance contract, and that's the tax you pay. This is also commonly referred to as "use tax."

What's the Difference?

Here's a quick sample of what the difference is between the two methods and an estimate of the potential gains by doing performance contracts and paying use tax instead of sales tax.

Let's say we have a customer that is willing to pay $25,000 for their kitchen job. Check out the difference between a sales tax model and a use tax model.

	Method 1 Sales Tax	Method 2 Use Tax
Total Sales	$25,000	$25,000
Sales Price of Taxable Goods	$21,000	$21,000
Sales Price of Labor (Non-Taxable)	$4,000	$4,000
Cost of Taxable Goods	$13,000	$13,000
Cost of Labor	$2,500	$2,500
Tax Paid (7%)	$1,470	$910
Total Cost	$16,970	$16,410
Gross Profit Margin $	$8,030	$8,590
Gross Profit Margin %	32.12%	34.36%
Dollars Gained $		$560
Profit % Gained		2.24%

So here you see that by doing nothing more than adopting the performance tax method of accounting for the sale, we added MORE THAN 2 PERCENT POINTS TO MARGIN AND GAINED $560! (Sorry for yelling, but this is significant for doing basically nothing.)

This means that for every $1 million in sales of these types of jobs, you would put $22,400 in your pocket.

OR, you could sell your jobs cheaper and be more competitive if you didn't want to keep the difference for yourself.

So what's the catch? Well there is one thing. You just have to pay tax of the cost of goods sold instead of the sales price of the job. This usually requires some better tracking and a detailed understanding of your job costs. Some companies find it easier to do it that way anyway, but if it's new to you, you may need some guidance.

Summary

I don't believe there is any easier way in the market today to make such an immediate impact on your bottom line. It baffles my mind why more dealers don't do it. I think it's because they just don't know about it.

Check your local tax laws and consult with your tax advisor to confirm these savings can be had in the states where you operate, or to see if there are specific exceptions in your area.

19

Why Dealers Switch Lines

2009/9/18 We get a lot of questions from dealers who are changing their product lines. They might be looking for a new niche product, but most of the time they switch for other reasons. And their number one question seems always to be:

Who's the easiest to do business with?

Over the years, we've dealt with hundreds of dealers. We find it interesting to track the reasons why dealers switch lines. It's not a comprehensive study by any stretch of the imagination, but it is very telling. Here's a summary of the results:

Reason	% Cases
Too Expensive to do business with	48%
Too difficult to do business with/Don't Like them	23%
Not selling enough / poor price / poor quality	12%
Manufacturer went direct / setup dealer in my area	9%
Other (market shift, closing location, etc)	8%

Seventy percent of the dealers switched lines for reasons the manufacturer could have avoided. Below is a summary of the common complaints in each area.

Too expensive to do business with—common complaints in this area are:

- The manufacturer makes me do their data entry or I have too much cost in my purchasing department.
- The manufacturer's credit/refund process is too painful or time consuming.
- I get billed incorrectly too many times.
- The manufacturer tries to get me to pay for mistakes that THEY make, including ordering and quality issues.
- My salespeople make too many pricing mistakes because their pricing is too complex/doesn't make sense.
- Their catalogs have too many errors, which costs me money.

Too difficult to do business with/don't like them—common complaints in this area are:

- The manufacturer grew too fast and lost the personal touch.
- You can't talk to a decision maker anymore.
- It takes too much effort to solve simple issues.
- Reps are poor quality or simply not available.

- The manufacturer is too internally focused.
- They give me too much stress/too many headaches.

It's Not Just about Quality and Price

When you sit back and look at what is really happening, it's easy to see that a dealer predominately drops a manufacturer line because:

- The processes between the dealer and manufacturer create extra costs.
- Emotionally the dealer feels neglected in some way.

While quality and cost will always remain a factor when a dealer drops a line, it pales in comparison to the many other reasons dealers drop lines.

There's an important point to drive home here. It's not the cost and quality of the product that predominantly makes the dealer unhappy over time. Remember, they would not have added the line to begin with if the price/cost weren't a fit. In addition to this, the dealer has spent time and money on their showroom to add the new line, as well as a new process (or two) to keep operations running smoothly. Overall, the act of switching a line is a hard emotional hurdle to get over for a dealer.

But if the manufacturer erodes the profitability of the dealership (e.g., ordering mistakes, pricing mistakes, excess rush fees, incorrect billing, etc.) dealers leave for greener pastures.

So if a dealer rarely drops a line because of product or price, isn't it strange that a manufacturer's primary focus is their product? Now obviously the product is important—after all it's what is being sold to the consumer. So it has to deliver on its promise. But the dealer isn't ultimately buying the manufacturer's product—the consumer is.

What a Dealer is Really Buying

The dealer is predominantly buying the manufacturer's ability to:
- Solve issues
- Help the dealer make a profit
- Make the overall experience of doing business with them incredibly easy, enjoyable, and rewarding for the dealer—both emotionally and financially

How Manufacturers Can Distinguish Themselves in the "Sea of Sameness"

I'm sure we've all heard dealers at some point say, "A cabinet is a cabinet is a cabinet," right? It's no exaggeration that many cabinet dealers describe a cabinet as a commodity—a product that every cabinet manufacturer thinks is different, but in reality is relatively the same in the dealer's eyes (except for that silly product code thing). Why? Because each manufacturer's process is just about as painful as the next, and this "pain" steals the thunder away from any truly unique product attribute. You can have the snazziest looking product of them all, but if you're not easy to do business with, nobody really cares.

Cabinet manufacturers have long struggled to distinguish themselves in what we refer to as "the sea of sameness." And they'll continue to struggle so long as their focus is on product alone. So here are our top ten things (plus two to grow on) a manufacturer can do to dramatically reduce the possibilities of getting dropped next time around:

1. Re-engineer your business process (credit, ordering, service, warranty, etc.) for the dealer's benefit, not yours.
2. Work with dealers to streamline and eliminate any excess or unnecessary costs.
3. Separate your design solutions from your pricing engine to achieve flexibility and ease in how you price your products.
4. Work with dealers to gather business intelligence on what sales promotions work best.
5. Invest in ways beyond just product training to help teach dealers to sell more effectively.

6. Stop forcing dealers to order "your way." Instead, build your systems around accepting dealer's orders "their way."

7. Invest in new tools to help you quickly rollout promotions, products, and new pricing.

8. If you make a mistake on your end, do the right thing and eat it for the dealer.

9. Focus on equipping dealers with tools, training, and best practices to make them more profitable and successful.

10. Make your pricing so simple that a fifth grader could do it.

11. Use your relationships and savvy to bring dealers more sales opportunities.

12. Remember that sometimes the executive (not the rep) just has to place that call with the dealer to let them know you are on top of the issue and that you truly appreciate their business.

I could go on for another twenty more, but I've always believed you should pick one, solve it, and then go to the next one. That's because as the old saying goes, actions really do speak louder than words—especially in this market.

Think of it this way, if you start today and knock out one a month, by this time next year you'll be the most sought after cabinet manufacturer on the planet.

20

How to Lose a Dealer in One Hour or Less

2009/10/2 Why do so many manufacturers give up millions long-term to get thousands short-term? It's happening all the time, and has been for years, but I still don't get it.

Here's the typical scenario: A dealer sells a manufacturer's line and they are building a good relationship together. Sales in that line are growing consistently, even to the point where that manufacturer's share of the overall dealer's business is increasing. It's a dealer for life, really, with the later years scheduled to deliver large amounts of value for both the dealer and the manufacturer.

In the midst of this positive momentum, an interesting phenomenon happens. A builder, contractor, dealer, or some other opportunity presents itself to the manufacturer where they can make a deal and get more money immediately. It could be in the form of any of the following:

- A builder or contractor wants to buy direct (with whom the dealer may or may not be focused on winning business).
- The manufacturer wants to set up another dealer that's "far enough away" from the original dealer (but close enough that the dealer, of course, gets upset).
- Any deal where the manufacturer finds itself saying these dangerous words: "Well, the dealer wouldn't be able to get the business anyway."

Someone Forgot His/Her Sales 101 Lessons

If you've ever read Stephen Covey's famous book *The Seven Habits of Highly Effective People,* he talks about the "emotional bank account." Rewarding actions build the emotional bank account in the form of "deposits" and non-rewarding actions make "withdrawals" from the emotional bank account. Too many withdrawals leave the bank account empty, resulting in a failed relationship.

I think sometimes manufacturers think the example above is a minor "withdrawal" from a dealer's emotional bank account—something that can easily be recovered in the future. A minor "bump" in the road.

What they don't realize is this is more like a devastating bankruptcy—the complete withdrawal of ALL deposits made up to this point. It's the ultimate sin of the dealer channel, really. In the mind of the dealer, that manufacturer is evil, and the dealer will never do business with them again.

The Results Are In

So let's review a summary of short-term and long-term results of this scenario:

Short-term Results
- Some revenue was generated for the manufacturer.

Long Term Results:
- The dealer's emotional bank account is officially empty.
- Any chance at long-term revenue is eliminated.
- Dealer is now actively putting a strategy in place to retire the manufacturer's line – permanently
- The dealer is now going out of their way to bad-mouth the manufacturer to all the other dealers— at networking events, industry venues, and any other event they can get their hands on.
- Since everyone knows the story, the manufacturer's competitors are using this in their sales calls to

help distinguish themselves as different—and going out of their way to visit that manufacturer's other dealers to tell the horror story (these kinds of events spread like wild-fire).

- The manufacturer's reps are effectively handicapped because this act portrays them as predators disguised to steal any new prospect's volume directly.

It's hard to imagine the logic that leads to this scenario, but the sheer quantity of these events makes us have to write about it. I think we can all see how the manufacturer's long-term relationship with that dealer is now ended—even if orders are still being placed months from now.

But eliminating that line at the dealer's site takes time—sometimes longer than a year. By then the manufacturer has long forgotten about it and simply sees a slowly declining revenue stream, and can't figure out why.

Wait, it Actually Gets Worse

The customer the manufacturer just obtained has absolutely no loyalty to the manufacturer. Typically the reason there is a deal like this to begin with is because the builder or other company is looking for a price the dealer can't give them. That's why the manufacturer is now involved. By nature, these are the deals that come with no loyalty because the customer is driven solely on price and will switch to a cheaper alternative as soon as the opportunity presents itself.

Worse yet, the manufacturer eroded the perceived value of their product in the surrounding marketplace by offering it at such a deep discount. The new direct customer spreads word that the manufacturer will wheel and deal, other dealers soon get negatively affected as some of their prospects and customers jump into the fray, and the manufacturer is forced through market pressure to lower prices even further. And so the downward spiraling saga continues....

The Summary

In just about every one of these cases, you can just look at the math and clearly see the manufacturer would have been financially much better off if they would've kept the relationship with the dealer. Or better yet, worked the dealer into the deal somehow.

I bet that on the wall of every person heading up a manufacturer's dealer channel is something that starts like:
- *"Our mission is to be the #1..."*

But most don't realize that there's only one way to actually pull this off. You have to win a dealer's loyalty more than all the other manufacturers do. And that's only done in small, consistent deposits into a dealer's emotional bank account.

Year after year after year.

CompanionCabinet Software

21

Sales Issues in the Kitchen and Bath Industry

Dictionary.com defines a professional as someone who is "engaged in one of the learned professions: a lawyer is a professional person." It takes three years to become a lawyer, yet it takes longer than that to learn how to be a kitchen and bath designer. Designers *are* professionals.

Kitchen Designer Requirements

Think of the knowledge required to design a kitchen. The average semi-custom cabinet manufacturer has more than five thousand products, with forty finish options and more than 150 potential modifications. But having access to such a depth of product doesn't really do anything for the consumer until a designer helps them to understand how it can be applied to creating a kitchen that is functional and supports their lifestyle. And even then, designing an efficient kitchen isn't enough. The style of the kitchen has to fit the house and spark a little envy when friends come to visit. It isn't easy.

The demands of the job itself are even greater. Designers not only need to be expert project managers, but must also be able to select the right materials for their designs, as well as the right professional installation crew to make their clients happy. It takes a long time to become a product expert, efficiency engineer, interior designer, and logistics expert. Kitchen and bath design is certainly a learned profession.

So why aren't kitchen designers treated with the same respect and professionalism as other professions? Lawyers don't have clients asking them for a contract that is then used to obtain a lower quote from another lawyer. Accountants are boring, yet they don't have to fight to get a return phone call. Why don't designers seem to get the same respect?

Big-box retailers have a lot to do with it. You don't see lawyers sitting in the middle of fifty thousand-square-foot stores writing contracts for anyone who walks up and asks for one. The ease with which prospective clients can get simple designs and a general lack of knowledge among consumers about how to recognize a premium design make it difficult for kitchen and bath designers to get the respect they deserve.

This is too bad. A kitchen remodel is one of the biggest investments a consumer will make in their lifetime. There are a lot of trade-offs to be considered and knowledge that needs to be shared. A third of the people who remodel their kitchen wish they had done something different after the project is completed. Perhaps the situation would have been different if a designer had helped them.

The average consumer considers a kitchen remodel for two and a half years before actually paying for it. They think about their needs, investigate products, and try to understand the unique features of each brand. It's only after doing this research that they feel comfortable sitting down with a designer. They think they know what they want, but need a professional to help make their vision come true. As a result, the designer becomes the critical link to their getting what they want.

Additional Responsibilities

In addition to product experts, efficiency engineers, interior designers, and logistics experts, designers have to serve, on occasion, as marriage counselors and financial advisors. Anyone who has seen a husband and wife debate budget and design knows this well. As a result, kitchen and bath design is a profession that requires unique talent, training, and a variety of skills.

Yet why don't consumers give designers the respect they deserve? What would happen if they did? Would designers sell more? Have you ever noticed that the designers who sell the most have a way of gaining the consumer's respect? Can most designers command the same level of respect and the corresponding sales volume? The answer is yes!

In 2008, there was a gathering of successful cabinet dealers to discuss the issues that affected the industry and to debate different solutions. One question generated more emotional debate than all the others combined: "How do I get great designers to sell more effectively?" The dealers discovered that each of them had a few great designers who were also very effective salespeople. These designers had certain ways of dealing with prospects that made the latter want to do business with them. A curiosity fell across the room. What were these high-sales-volume designers doing that was so different? Why were they able to sell more than their counterparts? Everyone agreed this couldn't be explained by the quality of their designs, which were good, but not that much better. It had to be something else.

The dealers agreed that they wanted to know what distinguished these designers who were natural-born salespeople from their peers. They arranged for their top-selling designers to be interviewed by a sales process expert and agreed to share their findings with the group.

The Naturals

The interviews soon revealed that the designers who displayed natural talent for sales had a much different way of dealing with prospects. They were not afraid to ask about budget, decision timeframes, or the sale. Even more curious were the similar rules each of them used to deal with their clients. These were rules that most of them didn't even know they were establishing. They just thought their unique manner of dealing with prospective clients was common. As a matter of fact, when they discovered that not everyone dealt with prospects as they did, they couldn't understand why.

The truth is that the designers with natural sales skills didn't do anything that was outrageously different. What was surprising, however, was that they all employed three unique techniques to sell prospects and shared similar views on how best to make a sale.

When the sales process expert shared his findings with the group, the dealers all had the same questions: "Can you teach others how to do what high-sales-volume designers do naturally?" The answer was yes. However, the sales techniques needed to be organized into a simple process that was easy to teach and easy for managers to reinforce.

Thus, the *4M Sales Process* was born.

Natural Process

Designers with natural sales ability position themselves as trusted experts who should be listened to and valued. Although the specific words that each designer uses may differ, their processes are the same. For example, when engaging a prospect for the first time, they are not preoccupied with what the prospect wants to buy but, instead, focus on making a connection. They know that to influence a prospect, they must show that they are trustworthy. To break down the trust barrier, they talk about a common experience—often family, organizations or interests—that they share with the prospect to build a foundation for their new relationship.

Unlike many of their peers, these designers also don't conduct a showroom "show and tell." They ask questions, listen, present new ideas, and wait for the prospect to talk. Their way of selling is more about discovering what the prospect wants to buy (and why) rather than about trying to sell.

Natural salespeople also focus on being likable. They let the prospect know they are a valuable resource and share stories about similar kitchens they have remodeled and how much the customers enjoyed the result. They are quick to talk in detail about how their company is uniquely positioned to benefit the prospect. They don't sell; they converse.

Another interesting technique they use is making and asking for commitments. These designers communicate clearly that they will exert effort on a potential client's behalf, but ask for the same in return. For example, when creating a design, they let the prospect know, in a very friendly way, that a timely decision is expected in exchange for the hours spent on crafting a solution that captures the prospect's vision.

Salesperson's Image

Top-selling designers manage their image quite well. They are always responsive to prospective clients, but not too responsive. They let it be known that they are in demand and that a prospect who wants to stay at the top of their priority list must make a commitment and maintain communication. If a prospect fails to do one or the other, these designers will not pursue them, but instead, focus their time on another, more promising client.

There's another way that designers with natural sales abilities distinguish themselves, which may seem minor, but can have a huge impact on effectiveness. They tell stories rather than recite cold, hard facts. Their stories are livelier, more interesting, and more relevant. When a potential client talks about a problem, these high-revenue designers use their concerns to set the stage for sharing an experience that shows they can help.

The manner in which the story is told is interesting as well. The story usually features people to whom the prospect can relate and whose problems are very similar. This similarity draws the prospect into the story and engages their emotions. Then a product or design feature is introduced and the characters' enjoyment of the benefit is discussed. This engages the prospect.

Relevant and interesting stories are the main tool of the designer who naturally sells well, which makes sense. Facts and figures are hard to remember and to relate to, while more personal accounts about people who are like you and who face the same challenges that you do but are now enjoying the benefits you desire, are far more memorable.

Presenting

Top-selling designers present their designs differently. They follow a process that makes them stand out from the competition, which begins at the moment the prospect walks in the door. After greeting the prospect, these designers will take them on a tour, introducing them to all the people at the dealership, including the receptionist, warehouse manager, installation manager, and finance manager. They make a point of conveying to the prospect that these managers are interested in them and want to ensure their experience with the company is a good one.

Next, both designer and customer spend a little time in the showroom. The designer shows the prospect some of the accessories that might be used in the design and tries to get a feel for the latter's interest level. Doing this also ensures that when a soft-close drawer or lazy Susan is suggested later, the prospect has a fresh memory of the item.

From the beginning, designers who have a knack for selling spend more time talking about the problems they are trying to solve and making sure they have uncovered all of the prospect's concerns.

The Design

When top-selling designers reveal their designs, they don't talk much. Instead, they ask the prospective client for their thoughts. A conversation ensues, during which the customer is encouraged to speak frankly. The features of the design are discussed and the prospect is asked to speculate on benefits. After the discussions, these designers will then confirm that the solution presented addresses the problems that they just reviewed.

As part of the process, the designers share plenty of stories. These cover everything from how specific features work and how the construction process will progress to stories that encourage the potential client to discuss their feelings. At the conclusion of the meeting, the customer is almost always sold. They also expect to be writing a check. And they are happy to do so.

Why would a prospect expect to write a check at the end of the design presentation? Well, because these designers set that expectation early on in the sales process. After all, they are comfortable establishing rules and expectations. Furthermore, they don't get mad at prospects who behave badly. They know that most prospects who treat them poorly do so because they just don't know any better, never having undertaken a kitchen remodel before. Consequently, top-selling designers are quick to explain the rules.

The rules aren't complex. They are based on common courtesy. Designers who are natural salespeople share with their prospects that they expect mutual respect and that once both parties make a commitment, they can count on one another to keep it.

These designers maintain a "win-win" or "no-deal" attitude. As a result, they make it clear to the prospect that they would rather lose the sale than agree to a term that one of the parties will someday regret. This lack of pressure creates trust. Therefore, one of the biggest and most important demands that these designers make is for the prospect to trust that honest, open, and timely feedback benefits both of them. With that in mind, they would rather that the prospect tell them "no" today than string them along. It hurts to hear no, but it also provides an opportunity to ask why. When objections surface, concerns can be addressed, and often the sale will be saved.

Teaching the Process

The cabinet dealers were impressed with what the sales process expert discovered. They quickly pressed him to tell them how to teach others how to sell in the same way. The result is CompanionCabinet's *4M Sales Process*. The process takes all the best practices of the designers who sell naturally and synthesizes them into a step-by-step process that can be taught to any designer.

Success in Selling

CompanionCabinet's *4M Sales Process* ensures anyone can learn salesmanship to generate as much as or more revenue than natural salespeople. Learned salesmanship is more consistently effective at winning deals and offers a quicker path to management for those who apply themselves.

But it all begins with learning the process. The 4M Steps include:

Meet. The designer learns how to establish rapport and trust quickly when first meeting a prospect. They also learn how to qualify the prospect and position themselves as experts. From this position of authority, it is easier for the designer to establish next steps and create rules that define the relationship with the prospect.

Measure. The designer measures the home and is given a set of techniques to gather information. These techniques help position the designers as the preferred vendor. The prospect will be impressed with the designer's skills, curious about their kitchen design ideas and certain that the designer is the person they want to have remodel their kitchen.

Match. The designer learns to reveal their design to the prospect in a unique way. This unusual technique gets the prospect involved in the presentation early and creates an environment where the prospect literally sells himself on doing business with the designer.

Make the Deal. When the designer meets with the prospect at this step in the process, they will have won the business 95 percent of the time. The designer learns special techniques to deal with price-sensitive prospects, last-minute competition, and unmotivated buyers.

A Story about Our Industry

The following pages contain a story that paints a picture that is very common in the cabinet industry. It's about Carl Jankon, a typical cabinet dealer owner. We wrote this in 1998 so manufacturers, reps and others could better understand a cabinet dealer's challenges.

It is modeled after a story about my father, Bob Jackson, who started his cabinet dealership back in 1963. As I grew up, I saw how hard he struggled. After I graduated college I ran from the cabinet business as fast as my feet would carry me, but like many of you, I ended up later coming back to the family business.

I hated watching what my dad had to go through to build his business – so many long hours, always surrounded by work and plagued by problems. After seeing this day in and day out, I developed a strong desire to find a way to improve the lives of every cabinet dealer – large or small.

In 1997 my closest friend and I began a dream to revolutionize the cabinet industry. We wanted to do something so unique and so effective it would forever change its landscape. Today, I am proud to announce the fulfillment of that dream.

The new world is finally here.

CompanionCabinet Software

With over 12 years of user input and feedback, we've launched something truly revolutionary. And all you need is an open mind. Well, and few minutes to go check out www.thinkcompanion.com. I promise you – it will forever change the way you operate in the cabinet industry.

Sincerely,

Brent Jackson, President, CompanionCabinet Software, LLC

Carl got up from his desk and walked out back by the pond. He needed a break. It was a warm summer morning and he drew a deep breath as he sat down. He stared out across the small pond. It was one of his few breaks throughout the day that he could justify.

He slowly let his mind wander, forgetting the craziness of the morning for just a few minutes...

It was raining when Carl Jankon and his friends graduated high school in 1960. There was quietness in the air that suppressed the excitement of the day. Carl's friends sat all around him. Some of them were headed off to college and others were headed off to start their jobs. Carl wished he could go to college. But no matter how many times he played with the numbers to try to make it all work, it just never added up.

He had just married his beautiful wife Jackie and she was expecting. Little Emily was just 2 months away. He was completely in love with his wife, the kind of relationship you only see in the movies. Carl was 18 and was already a skilled cabinet installer for a local cabinet dealer.

Carl knew a lot about installing cabinets. He learned it all from his Dad. Everyone around him respected him for his work. He did whatever it took to get the job done. He was a craftsman at heart. Times were tough, but he was tougher. It didn't matter if a job was cancelled that day either – he'd just go downtown and pick up any random job to make ends meet. If that meant working through the night, then that's what he did. His bills would be paid and his family would always be taken care of – no matter what the personal cost. It's just the mold he was cut from.

After the first few years of installing cabinets, it became apparent that Carl was very skilled and a natural leader. He was quickly promoted to be the installation manager over 8 other installers. He received a salary, some incentives and more responsibility. He moved out of his cramped apartment with Jackie and Emily and purchased a small house close to the cabinet shop. This way he could have a shorter drive home. His days were hectic, and after about 6pm he retired back to his office to start on the paperwork for the next day's activities. The personal computer wouldn't be invented until 1981. Pencil and paper ruled the day. He usually made it home by 9pm.

Carl's first 5 years went by quickly. He worked late into the evenings and returned home most of the time after Emily was asleep. It felt to him like he was never able to see her much. He worried often that he was missing Emily's childhood. He took some comfort in the fact that she had a roof over her head, clothing and food. It was difficult to save much with his salary, and Carl wasn't able to take many vacations. He often offered to work over the holidays for extra money.

The cabinet shop was called Finkleton Lumber. They sold all sorts of things besides cabinets. The Finkletons had owned it for as long as Carl could remember. John Finkleton was getting old and rumor had it he wanted to sell the business. Late into the evenings Carl would often muse about the idea of owning the business. Of course you had to have money to do that and Carl was a realist at heart. He thought it was fun to dream about, though.

The rumor of John wanting to sell the business continued over the next 6 years. In that time, Carl was promoted three more times. By 1971, Carl was head of operations for Finkleton Lumber. He and John sat in many meetings together talking about the company's performance and ways they could better serve their customers.

One day, in the summer of 1971, John and Carl were driving together to quiet an angry customer. It was Amory Homes, a larger builder that they had done a lot of work with over the years. Apparently, many things had gone wrong on the job site.

"Tell me what happened, Carl" asked John.

"Well. It's a long list of things we did wrong. You know how the paperwork is. Things got confused – and I mean really confused. And we didn't catch it in time. Seems like we're doing that a lot these days."

John's eyes squinted in the afternoon sun, a pained expression on his face. "What do you think we should do?" asked John, listening quietly.

Carl sat for a moment before responding. It was the first time John had asked him this. Usually Carl was the one to just listen and make it happen. "Well, for starters," Carl answered hesitantly, "Kevin is the owner of Amory and he's a no nonsense guy. He gets angry, but mainly when he thinks you're not being honest with him."

"Go on," said John.

"Well, if I were in your shoes," said Carl, gaining confidence, "I'd tell him we screwed up and we'll make it right no matter what the cost. His repeat business is worth way more than this one job. Then I'd spend the meeting telling him about the next steps of how we will correct this so he knows we are on it. Then I think he'll be fine."

John smiled. He felt as if the weight of the world had been lifted from his shoulders. Finally, he thought, someone to take over after he retires. He had a long line of potential successors, but he was concerned about how they would carry on his legacy. He wanted someone to take over that would care for his customers and treat them right. He knew Carl had that spark that kept customers coming back. And they trusted him.

"Carl," John said, "You and I have a lot to talk about after this meeting".

Carl didn't know quite what to think.

By 1995, Jankon Cabinets & Countertops was the dominate dealer in Charlotte, NC. Carl had opened up two more retail locations since buying the business in 1972. They were now approaching $10M in sales. It had all happened so fast.

There was no time to enjoy the progress, however — things were busier than ever. Carl was 55 now. He had put on some weight and the stress was getting to him. His Nextel beeped every few minutes like some endless alarm and it seemed like there was always a fire to put out. In this business, Carl thought, retail customers were never happy. At best, you could manage down their expectations and eliminate some common mistakes — but mostly you were lucky if a job went right and a customer actually came back a second time. When the customers were happy, it was through sheer force of will and salesperson heroics. Like the guy juggling all those dishes — it promised to be a mess to clean up later but every once in a while he didn't drop one.

Carl had purchased the business from John and he remembered how excited he and his wife Jackie were. He was his own boss and after their second child, he felt like he was on top of the world. But within just a few years, he felt like he was buried underneath it. The sheer quantity of things to deal with was overwhelming. Besides the seeming endless job completion issues they struggled

CompanionCabinet Software

with, he had all the challenges of running a successful cabinet dealership.

Carl had aged quickly. He didn't feel healthy. He didn't get much time to exercise these days. Most of his business debt from the buyout was gone, but now all of his money was tied up in inventory. Business was strong and cash flow was strong, but he knew they were losing money in many areas of the business. The problem was that he had no clear information about where they were losing it. Everything was done on instinct and every location seemed to do business slightly differently.

He didn't have time to cover all the locations. He worried that he had spread himself too thin. Everyone seemed busy and productive with all those new computers they had purchased, but strangely enough, pencil and paper still ruled the day. He never did understand those things – but everyone swore by them. He just wished they could somehow help his people sell more and show him some decent information about his business so he could make better decisions. Like which salespeople were killing it? Which ones needed to be let go? Which customers were causing him the majority of his headaches? He could guess a few, but he worried that much of the real issues were buried in paper job folders in someone's trunk.

Sometimes he would look down the hallway at his office and shake his head at all the copy machines and filing cabinets. He didn't have enough space to keep all that paper — much of it was starting to go offsite now. It was crazy to him that he had to rent space just to store the paper. Wasted money, really. But you never knew when you would need that job file for some warranty claim.

Sometimes, late into the evening, he would go through the salespeople's older job folders, looking for problems. It would take hours but he was always able to find a mistake. $50 here, $150 there. It made him sick. A cabinet someone priced wrong, some hardware someone forgot to charge for, a service ticket that should have been billed but was forgotten. Carl was convinced that the places where you could lose money in the cabinet business were endless. No matter how hard he tried to remind everyone, they made the same mistakes — year after year.

He felt like things could be so much better — that he could be making so much more money. Keeping the business moving was an incredible feat of will. It just always felt to him like he was swimming upstream. The cabinet business was so exhausting, but not many people could make money at it like he could.

CompanionCabinet Software

Despite his uncanny ability to make money, Carl was already starting to think of getting out of the rat race and doing what John had done to him.

Carl was tired and his wife was too. She had joined the business when they bought it and helped out in the purchasing and accounting department. He knew that if he thought he had it bad, Jackie must have it ten times worse. Billing and purchasing was a nightmare.

They had eight people in their purchasing department when they should have had one. It seemed like all they did all day was rekey orders into their other systems or into their manufacturer's ordering systems. It was the business of headaches, mistakes and excess labor. But after so many years of hoping for some magic solution, Carl eventually just accepted his lot in life.

Carl knew he was destined to grow old here - to spend the majority of his waking hours inside the store walls until he could retire. He had known it for years. He was the business. He had no son to take over. No daughter that wanted any part of it. And no one who would buy the paperwork house of cards he had built.

When he and his wife were done, the doors would close - permanently. Hopefully their savings would take them far enough. He thought they would if they were careful enough. It would be a simple and humble life, and he was okay with that. After all, many of his fellow dealers had gone under. He was just thankful that his business had survived. Eventually he would sell off the inventory when it was time, sell the building and start a hobby he wanted to do for quite some time now: fishing.

It was something where his mind could relax. A life where he and Jackie could relax. Something fun for a change.

Carl clenched his teeth and squinted his eyes. All that would have to wait for now. He slowly stood up and made his way back to the warehouse. Tonight there was going to be a lot of paperwork to catch up on.

He'd have to order dinner at the office...again.

CompanionCabinet Software

Our sponsors

Appendix-Afterword

As we began writing these articles I remember thinking that the cabinet industry is very simple. You find customers, provide them with great product, and make money in the process. The concept is simple, but executing it is tough. In this book, I shared insights into how to make your cabinet dealership more successful. I hope you found the ideas practical and actionable.

As a founder of CompanionCabinet software I have the opportunity to help cabinet dealers automate their businesses. As I work with these people in overcoming their most challenging problems, four key issues dominate our conversation. Dealers want to:

- Control margins – People need a way to ensure multiple sales people in different locations produce error free quotes at approved margins.
- Eliminate paperwork – Dealers want to be able to take a quote, convert it into multiple purchase orders, and place error-free orders with the manufacturers, without any re-typing.
- Enhance customer responsiveness – Salespeople and customer service staff need to be able to locate information quickly in active and archived job files when customers want answers.

- Gain control – Business owners need to get accurate and timely sales, cost, and profitability information by job, customer, and salesperson.

My experience is that when these four issues go unaddressed, owners stay up late at night either trying to anticipate tomorrow's problems or worrying about money. In 1997, my business partner and I began building software that tackles these issues. Today we call it Aurora.

Aurora was modeled after best practices from thousands of operations. It doesn't require any hardware or complicated installs. You can roll it out 100X faster than traditional desktop software.

Aurora reads kitchen design files and then produces accurate quotes at management-determined margins. Once the quote is accepted, the software converts the quote into sales and purchase orders and, after approval, places the orders with the manufacturers electronically.

Multiple customer service people can quickly respond to customer questions by accessing information from a browser anywhere, anytime. Management can generate reports that show profit by job, salesperson, location and customer. The best way to summarize the software is that it is a comprehensive solution that puts you in complete control of your cabinet operation. To learn more visit www. thinkcompanion.com or call us at 704-688-4090.

If you have any questions about our software, or if I can be helpful to you in anyway, please feel free to contact me personally, by email or phone.

Brent Jackson, President, CompanionCabinet Software, LLC

Made in the USA
Charleston, SC
13 December 2011